Impact

A Novella

By

DAVID GLEDHILL

ISBN-13: 978-1541371552

ISBN-10: 1541371550

DEDICATION

This book is dedicated to all those who lost their lives in the service of their Country on the ground and in the air.

CONTENTS

	Prologue. The North German Plain Near Osnabruck, December 1983.	1
1	The Officers' Married Quarters, RAF Wildenrath on the Dutch Border, the previous night.	4
2	The Officers' Married Quarters, Wassenberg Village, the previous night.	8
3	Off the Welsh Coast, 0710 hours.	10
4	The Officers' Mess, RAF Brüggen on the Dutch Border.	14
5	Delta Dispersal, RAF Wildenrath.	16
6	The Officers' Mess, RAF Brüggen.	19
7	Delta Dispersal, RAF Wildenrath.	25
8	The Pilots' Briefing Facility, Alpha Dispersal, RAF Brüggen.	28
9	The 92 Squadron Aircrew Crewroom, Delta Dispersal, RAF Wildenrath.	32
10	Alpha Dispersal, RAF Brüggen.	34
11	The 92 Squadron Operations Room, RAF Wildenrath.	36
12	Alpha Dispersal, RAF Brüggen.	39
13	The 92 Squadron Briefing Room, RAF Wildenrath.	42
14	Hardened Aircraft Shelter 24, RAF Brüggen.	56
15	Delta Dispersal, RAF Wildenrath.	63
16	Fifteen Minutes to Impact.	65
17	Ten Minutes to Impact.	68
18	Five Minutes to Impact.	77
19	Three Minutes to Impact.	81

20	One Minutes to Impact.	83
21	Thirty Seconds to Impact.	85
22	Impact.	87
	Epilogue.	94
	About the Author	98
	Author's Note.	99
	Glossary.	101
	Other Books By This Author.	106

PROLOGUE

The North German Plain Near Osnabruck, December 1983.

The search and rescue helicopter clattered across the tree line and alighted in the centre of the meadow stirring up a cloud of fallen leaves and debris. The moment the rotors had braked to a halt the cabin door drew back and the crew and passengers disgorged into the lee of the cabin, the recent solitude a faint memory. The noise of the engine was replaced by the whine of an auxiliary power unit, the incessant bleep of an emergency locator beacon emanating from the cockpit marking a rhythm.

Packs were hastily stacked at the base of a tree as the men made preparations to seal the site. An NCO barked a few brief orders and the team fanned out to the peripheries. Two guards moved swiftly to a barred gate climbing the stout structure which sealed the only entrance taking up station on the far side.

The ugly gouge which scarred the tranquil glade stretched the length of the field from the stark gap in the trees to a still smoking crater. Debris littered the deep furrow with shards of metal that had once been a combat jet. Rising above the crater was the unmistakable profile of the rear fuselage, the afterburner petals of the jet pipes forming perfect circles in contrast to the straight lines around. Little else marked the fact that this had, until minutes before, been one of the most powerful symbols of man's ability to wreak destruction. That it had met its demise in such a tranquil and pretty spot was the ultimate irony.

The NCO walked quickly to the crater. He had been given two simple tasks at the hastily arranged briefing back at base; firstly to secure the site which he would achieve swiftly and, secondly, to find the pilot. Surveying the angle at which the jet had struck the ground, if the poor man or men, were still in the cockpit and he had no idea of the identity of the jet as yet, there was no hope of survival. Although it was a miracle that the entire airframe had not disintegrated there was little left of the area forward of the main wing box and certainly nothing that resembled a cockpit. Scanning backwards along the trench he picked out two larger pieces of wreckage which were obviously the tailplane. A jagged section of the fin resplendent with the squadron markings identified the unit from which it had come and his heart sank. It lay at an impossible angle in the furrow. Turning back to the hulk, the wings had, remarkably, remained attached but the flaps, released from their hydraulic grip, had relaxed and the wing line was broken. A wheel, untouched in the crash was visible through the undercarriage door which had cracked open. The main section was almost undamaged and the smooth belly of the once proud jet was still recognisable but the carnage forward of that area was complete. A bow wave of earth and grass sods had been fashioned ahead of the wreckage, testament to the forces which had subsided a short time ago. If the cockpit still existed it was buried beneath. More likely it formed part of the trail of broken parts strewn along the trench.

The distant shout was about to put paid to any hopes of a happy outcome. One of the hastily formed search party beckoned from the gate his gesture urgent, his voice strident. The NCO made his way over.

"We found the pilot Sarge."

The slight shake of the head left nothing to interpret and the pair set off along the narrow lane without further exchange. Rounding the bend, the jagged swathe cut in the trees by the doomed jet was stark against the horizon and the weak afternoon sun shone through the gap bathing the field in a suffused glow. A few metres away, a group of airman clustered around a small tree the object of their interest unrecognisable from this distance. As he closed on the scene he passed the Martin Baker ejection seat lying on its back on the ground; an empty shell.

The chance of survival had been illusory. Although the ejection seat had propelled its occupant away from the doomed jet, it had struck the trunk of a tree, seemingly a fluke of circumstance given the wide open spaces around. Chillingly, the trajectory had been downwards and there had been no time for the automatics that controlled the seat to operate correctly. Although its mechanical sequence had begun, the handle had been pulled too late and too close to the ground to assure survival. The occupant had still been strapped in the seat when he struck the tree.

The body lay at the base of the trunk separated some distance from the seat but still joined by the tangle of parachute rigging and the parachute harness. His visor had dropped under the stress of ejecting, the dark visor hiding his dead eyes from his rescuers. He might yet have been resting but for the massive damage to his helmet hidden from casual scrutiny. The paraphernalia of survival gear designed to keep him alive seemed incongruous under the circumstances. The bright orange, white and green of the parachute canopy set vivid against the green foliage was hanging down from the branches, draped almost artistically. A bright yellow pack which housed the small rubber life raft, designed to protect, lay some distance away ejected from its snug housing in the ejection seat during the impact. The seat in turn lay some metres from the tree, its headbox mangled where it had struck the unyielding bark giving a horrific insight into the likely injuries which had claimed the pilot's life.

As a second helicopter adorned with bright red crosses alighted alongside the first, the NCO reflected that a mortuary team rather than a doctor was needed. He dispatched two more guards to close the road blocking access to the site. It would be closed for the foreseeable future.

CHAPTER 1

The Officers' Married Quarters, RAF Wildenrath on the Dutch Border, the previous night.

Squadron Leader "Mac" McKenzie stretched out on the uncomfortable service issue couch, the gaudy flowered pattern jarring his senses, listening to the familiar litany from his wife. An amiable Scot, slightly overweight with a florid complexion but otherwise healthy, he was the very essence of popularity on the Squadron. An experienced Phantom pilot, exceptional weapons instructor and generally all-round good bloke he was the epitome of the mantra "fight hard, play hard". His home life, however, was less prescribed and tonight's discussion was following the usual format. As soon as the children were in bed the complaints would begin about the school on base. The teachers, mostly young and personable single women, were distracted by their social life in the Officers' Mess, the facilities were cramped and inadequate, the curriculum was being poorly delivered and, obviously, all this was affecting the children's education. That their eldest was turning twelve with his incipient interest in girls growing might be a more relevant distraction seemed lost on his wife who was, otherwise shrewd in the ways of the world. He resigned himself to another round of earache when the conversation turned more serious.

"I mean it Alexander" - only his wife called him Alexander. "Justin is losing out being here in Germany. If I don't do something soon his preparation for his exams will be disrupted and he'll leave school without any relevant qualifications."

"Look, we've spoken about this at length, my love. We can look for a private tutor if you want. It'll focus his attention on the key subjects. He's bright at maths and his English grades are stellar. He'll settle down. It's early days yet."

"No it's not. We've been here a year and, if anything, his grades are getting worse. There's no option but to put him into boarding school."

"Look, we've talked about that too. How can we sort that from here? Far better to wait until I get my posting and then we'll find the right place to move him to, hopefully, closer to where I'm stationed."

Mac had been on the Squadron for twelve months and, as one of the Executives, had been given a thirty month tour of duty. It would be another year before he found out his future employment.

"It's twelve months before you find out where you're posted to and it could be anywhere from High Wycombe to Bentley Priory to Central London. How can we plan around that?"

He groaned at the ever revolving argument. They had discussed it endlessly without resolution and he was losing the will to discuss it further. No plan survived first contact with the enemy, in this case the poster at RAF Barnwood, but without an inkling as to where his next tour would be, almost certain to be a ground tour, he was stabbing in the dark. What he had not mentioned to his nearest and dearest was that, as the Weapons Leader on the Squadron, there was a strong possibility that he might be posted to the Strike Command Air-to-Air Missile Establishment to run that operation. The bad news was that STCAAME, as it was fondly known, was based on the remote island of Anglesey in West Wales. This posting might prove to be the death knell for their increasingly fragile marriage.

"You know I hate it here," she continued. "I resent having had to give up my job to move to this swamp. There are no jobs locally for someone like me who doesn't speak German and Lord knows I've looked. Even Hitler didn't station his troops here for longer than three months at a time because of the damp atmosphere. I detest the endless rounds of coffee mornings with wives who have little interest beyond their own babies. I'm slowly going mad."

The script was panning out in its usual predictable way. He couldn't understand her point of view. Most people at Wildenrath enjoyed the life style. Suddenly, the mood changed.

"No I've decided. I'm going back to UK. I won't be driven by the Air Force any more. Loyalty only goes so far."

"Do you mean what I think you mean Lucy? Are you suggesting we split up?"

"No silly. I'll move back in with my parents, temporarily, just until we find out where we'll be for the next tour. It will allow us to get Justin into public school and give us space to find a house somewhere. You can get back to UK regularly and then we can look at you commuting to your new job. A house somewhere in the London catchment will be well placed for any of the three likely jobs. Lord knows we can afford it. I've simply had it with Air Force married quarters. I need my own home again."

"But we have a good life here. The social scene is great and the local allowances make up a little for your loss of income. We live well."

"It's fine for you off at the Squadron all day but think about me. Once I pack the children off, all I can look forward to is a book or someone popping in for a chat. No I'm decided. I'll start to make arrangements straight away. I've already broached the idea with Mum and she's hugely supportive."

"Glad I was the first to know," he muttered darkly. "You know that means I'll have to move back into the Officers' Mess don't you? I'll be lucky if I survive the tour with two functioning kidneys."

The weak humour belied a serious point. Mac's life was about to change drastically and, in his eyes, not for the better. The frown was intense.

"I'm going to bed," he announced. "Let's talk about this again tomorrow."

A short time later he placed a reassuring hand on his wife's shoulder. The steady breathing may have been a bluff but either way, the lack of response was telling. He sighed and rolled over.

CHAPTER 2

The Officers' Married Quarters, Wassenberg Village, the previous night.

Flying Officer James Linton-Cockerham or "Cockers" to his friends, was typically ebullient. Newly married and living the dream, his attractive wife bustled around the kitchen preparing dinner.

One of the social elite, his public school upbringing had set him in good stead for his life at Wildenrath and the fact that his father, who was ex Household Cavalry, knew the Station Commander from their days at Staff College helped enormously. Any leg up the social hierarchy was to be nurtured and James could play the odds. Despite his charmed social status he was popular on the squadron and his roguish charm sat well with his confident, well if the truth be known, over confident air making him popular with his peers and commanders alike.

All was not quite rosy. After he had left the service his Father had moved into the City and joined the financial helter skelter. Although his initial gains had been spectacular, recent downturns had tempered the meteoric growth and the bubble had threatened to burst. Although James could not see it, an over optimistic Bull Market coupled with inflated property prices threatened the once inevitable inheritance windfall he was looking forward to and depending upon.

In the meantime he was enjoying the exciting ride and he watched his wife's delightful rear end as she placed plates in the oven ready for the evening meal. He had kicked off his flying boots which lay in a haphazard heap in the middle of the floor but he was still wearing his flying suit as he watched the evening news on the British Forces Broadcasting Service. It was the only English language TV channel in the area other than the occasional English movie on one of the Dutch TV channels but he was grateful for the distraction. The glass of sweet white German wine on the coffee table merely added to his contentment.

For his own part he was enjoying supporting the local economy. His first act on being posted-in had been to visit the local Commerzbank and arrange a sizeable loan to fund a new car purchase. His jet black VW Golf GTi was resplendently sitting outside in its parking spot. This very morning, he and his wife had dropped into the travel agents on base and booked their summer holiday in Monaco. It was a destination he had dreamed of visiting and the removal of the massive obstacle which was the English Channel meant he could now reach the French coast in little over twelve hours of high speed travel, mostly down the German autobahns and French autoroutes. That he could undertake almost the whole journey using duty free petrol was an added bonus. Once the news was over he would fire up their new Hi-fi and they would listen to some Dire Straits whilst they ate dinner. Life was, indeed, sweet.

He would not spoil the evening with distasteful discussions over finances. His wife was convinced that his imminent promotion to Flight Lieutenant would solved their slightly overstretched budget and that, in any event, his forthcoming inheritance could always be massaged to resolve immediate worries. In the meantime they would plan for this weekend's latest round of parties. In any case, tomorrow looked good. He was on the programme for an affiliation sortie with the F-104s from Jever. They would meet up in Low Flying Area 2 and it should be a good sortie if the weather proved as good as the forecast promised.

Yes life was indeed, very sweet.

CHAPTER 3

Off the Welsh Coast, 0710 Hours.

"Alpha turn left heading 220 and descend to 1,500 feet on the regional QNH 1024." instructed the range controller from the airfield at Aberporth Rangehead on the Ceredigion coast.

"Left 220 and descend to 1,500 feet, Alpha."

The Phantom eased onto its new heading with its pilot glued to the instruments making sure each of the pre-briefed parameters was precisely achieved; heading, height, speed.

"Minus three minutes."

"Minus three minutes, Alpha."

The clock was counting down inexorably to a rendezvous between the Jindivik target drone somewhere out there in Cardigan Bay with the Sparrow semi-active air-to-air missile slung in the housing below the rear fuselage.

"Contact with the target range two miles and closing. Target converging from the right and it should cross the nose at one mile. Stand by. Locking up," the navigator declared.

The radar scanner went into a mechanical gyration as the navigator squeezed the acquisition trigger around the fuzzy blip on the radar display. A moment of electronic hesitation before the full track symbology sprang into life and a raft of additional information flooded the screen.

"Good lock," the navigator breathed the relief evident in his voice.

"Playmate, flares now," came the disembodied voice of the controller.

"Visual."

"Your dot," the pilot heard from the back seat.

The pyrotechnic flares mounted in the tiny pod trailing behind the Jindivik drone burst into life providing an immediate visual reference from the incendiary payload which now trailed a plume of smoke in its wake. Tracing the line of the smoke forward the pilot could see the tiny red and yellow target as it began the gentle turn as briefed. He moved the control column gently to match the manoeuvre and check the drift. The radar which was tracking the target would provide the steering commands to the huge missile under the fuselage but if he allowed the target to drift off the side of the radar scope the radar would lose contact, break lock and the firing would be aborted.

"Minus 20 seconds."

The atmosphere in the cockpit was tense. The steering dot was firmly in the middle with the allowable steering error circle having expanded to its maximum value. It was just as he had been briefed it would be. Everything looked perfect.

"Minus ten seconds."

"Happy mate?" the pilot queried. The navigator checked the parameters; all good. He double checked the lock and the radar was tracking like a God; perfect.

"Affirmative, confirm CW is on, Sparrow selected and selected and ready lights illuminated."

It was the final housekeeping before the shot.

“Affirmative, all good in the front.”

“Happy in the back.”

“‘“5–4–3–2–1; punch; clear to fire.”

The controllers voice stepped up an octave sensing the tension of the event.

“Clear to fire, Alpha.”

There was a pause.

“Firing, firing, now!”

An electronic beep filled the frequency.

Another pause.

Whoooooooooooooooosshhhhhh.

The Sparrow left the rail with an audible thud as the hydraulic ram pushed it out into the disturbed airflow beneath the Phantom. For a moment it was invisible to the crew as the pilot eased up and turned gently away to give the chase camera ship a clear view but as he dropped the left wing, a distinct, white smoke trail snaked away from their flight path, a gyrating missile at its head. At such close range and with the missile travelling at Mach 2.8 over launch speed, the short distance to the target was covered in seconds.

"Bloody hell we got the Jindi!” the navigator exulted.

“That’ll cheer them up,” replied a slightly anxious pilot before realising that he had absolutely no control over its destiny in the cockpit. The small radar reflecting target on the drone and designed to protect against a direct hit had clearly failed to do its job. As he watched, the wreckage, which had until very recently been a Jindivik, struck the sea and disappeared rapidly from view.

“Caravan, offside,” he transmitted announcing the fate of the Jindivik to its distraught controller.

“Roger Alpha, vector 010 for Bardsey Island and contact Valley Approach on 264.7, good day Sir.”

"Roger to Valley Approach, good day."

After the loss of a Jindivik, a tense debrief would follow once the Phantom landed at STCAAME even though the firing had been faultless. The crew steeled themselves for the interrogation to come.

*

"Bloody marvellous!"

"What was that mate?"

"Nothing, just thinking back to the firing."

"It was pretty good fun wasn't it?"

"You can say that again."

The debrief had, surprisingly, gone smoothly with praise offered all round and, after a quick turn round at RAF Valley, they had been released to return home. The cockpit had been quiet since they had handed off from the UK air traffic agency to Dutch Military but they were now approaching the top of descent for their recovery to Wildenrath. Mark "Razor" Keene and Jim "Flash" Gordon were enjoying the quiet after the hectic events of the last few hours. The missile firing had come out of the blue. Normally no-notice firings were tasked to the crews on Battle Flight and the hooter would sound without warning heralding a mad dash to Wales and an unexpected missile launch. This time the powers that be had wanted a telemetered round fitted with sensors and relay gear to transmit data back to the ground for analysis. The tiny transmitter had been loaded into the Sparrow in the space normally occupied by the warhead, they had been quickly briefed on the profile and dispatched to the weapons range at Cardigan Bay. The firing had been faultless. They were winging their way back to Wildenrath and would be home before breakfast.

"RAFAIR 3452 begin your descent now, initially to 5,000 feet and contact Clutch Radar on Stud 13 for recovery, good day Sir."

CHAPTER 4

The Officers' Mess, RAF Brüggen on the Dutch Border.

As a first tour pilot, flying the single seat Jaguar in RAF Germany was the culmination of a life's ambition for Nick Gleason. Outwardly confident, good looking and popular with the resident teachers from the RAF school who shared the Officers' Mess, he seemed the epitome of the successful combat pilot. The reality was that, with pressures unseen to his colleagues and supervisors on the Squadron, he was becoming increasingly withdrawn and risked becoming a loner. The attractions of socialising in the Mess Bar in the evenings had waned and pouring himself into bed worse for wear every evening was taking its toll. He had promised himself that he would spend more time in the gym and work out for a skiing trip later in the year. He had been declared combat ready six months ago and by now he should be extending his horizons and visiting the undoubted attractions available to him on the Continent. He was tiring of listening to others tell tales of the interesting places they had visited and it was time to experience some of them for himself.

His lack of sightseeing was the least of his troubles, he thought dropping the letter from his sister into the drawer in his bedside cabinet. The news had come out of nowhere. She had only gone and joined the Greenham Common Peace Camp to protest against nuclear proliferation and with him being a bomber pilot holding nuclear quick reaction alert. His annual vetting with the security man was due in a few months time. If he failed to disclose this little nugget and it came out, which it undoubtedly would, his clearances would be pulled in an instant. He would have to fess up and the only question was when. Was it too much to hope she would see it as a passing phase and go home to their family? Knowing his sister, he doubted it. She was as persistent and dogmatic as he was.

That was not all. His first validation of his nuclear target planning was due this week. Not only would he be grilled on the contents of his target folder by his Flight Commander but he would be required to fly a practise profile selected to mirror the actual mission distances and timings. The flight was tomorrow and he was seriously behind with his preparation. His recent ride with the standardisation team, The "Trappers" from the Jaguar Operational Conversion Unit at Lossiemouth had been a nightmare. He should have done much better having only finished his conversion training last year but he had allowed the bright lights of Germany to divert his attention. His academic score for systems knowledge had been abysmal and he had only just scraped a pass.

He had a lot of work to do this week.

CHAPTER 5

Delta Dispersal, RAF Wildenrath.

The headlights cut a swathe through the pine trees that ringed the dispersal as Mac pulled his MGB Roadster into the car park. He was not the first to arrive and an RAF policeman was loading his German Shepherd into a dirty Ford Escort van, his shift guarding the dispersal over for another night. The engineering day shift had already been busy for well over an hour preparing the jets for the day's flying.

The courtesy light in the car alongside glowed dimly and he was vaguely aware of a torch beam scanning the ground under the vehicle.

"It's a bit early for security checks Keith."

A head popped up, the look on the owners face distracted and ill-tempered.

"Morning Sir," Flight Lieutenant Keith Willis replied, his service hat skewed on his head giving a faintly comic air. "Dropped my bloody car keys when I got out and I'm damned if I can find them."

"Hang on, I've got a torch here somewhere. I'll come and give you a hand."

Mac fumbled in the glove box and pulled out a Maglight he had picked up at the American BX during his last landaway at Bitburg. Twisting the tiny head a strong beam shone brightly. He dropped down on his haunches and began a square search under the car just in time to hear a contented grunt as the offending item was located.

"Got 'em."

Mac tucked the torch into his pocket. He had been meaning to put it into his "go pack" to replace the useless piece of kit the Air Force expected him to use. The official night flying torch boasted batteries that would power the Titanic, weighed a ton and looked like something from the battlefields of World War Two. It had no place in a fighter cockpit.

Across the dispersal, the slab sided pilot's briefing facility, or PBF in the vernacular, stood central to the complex its green walls illuminated by sodium lights on all sides. The two officers made their way past the barbed wire screens which had been drawn back from the entrance to the dispersal, threading through the narrow gap that restricted access to all but pedestrians and bicycles. A green, toned-down sangar, squat but brutally functional, lay just beyond the wire marking the transition from normal life to the operational area. During exercises it was the temporary home to the guards who protected the busy dispersal. For now its sheer presence was forbidding.

"Are you the Auth this morning?" asked Mac distracted by the sounds of the heavy clamshell doors of an adjacent hardened aircraft shelter as they swung open beneath the protective concrete canopy revealing a Phantom bathed in fluorescent light. The ugly profile of his current mount never failed to impress with its brutal functionality; the upturned wingtips and downturned stabilator unique amongst fighter designs. He could not suppress the sense of excitement he felt at the start of every. . . . . well most, working days.

"For my sins," replied the young Flight Lieutenant. "I think I must have upset the programmer. This is my third stint on "earlies" in the last two weeks. What with Battle Flight, I only seem to see this place at night. It's dark when I come into work and dark when I go home."

"Cheer up. The good thing about being on the desk is you can keep an eye out for the good deals when the programmer is writing tomorrow's schedule."

"Did I see you're down for the Buccaneer Affiliation sortie later?"

"Yes, Cockers is getting towards the end of his convex and I'll get him to plan and brief the intercepts today. It'll be good preparation for his Tac Check. As soon as we get him operational we can add him to the Battle Flight roster and take a bit of pressure off the rest of us."

"How's he doing?"

"Pretty good for an ab-initio. He's got a good head on his shoulders. A tad over confident if anything but, at this stage, maybe that's not such a bad thing. Just the routine of squadron life, once he's combat ready, will bring him down to earth."

"Amen to that," Willis replied.

They walked in through the doorway to the low wood-built annex, the lights welcoming. The first stop every morning, and this morning was no exception, was the coffee bar and that first shot of caffeine to bump start proceedings.

CHAPTER 6

The Officers' Mess RAF Brüggen.

Nick Gleason tossed uncomfortably, beads of sweat forming on his brow. The colours were vivid.

His Jaguar hugged the contours of an undulating plain, a city skyline dominating the horizon. The speed of the approach registered subconsciously as trees and telegraph poles flashed through his peripheral vision. On his wing some yards distant the sleek profile of a camouflaged Phantom travelled in silent company guarding his every move. A silent sentinel, detached and wraith-like.

His eyes were drawn to the symbols in his head up display that flashed, momentarily, the pull cue illuminating, prompting him to pull back on the stick. The Jaguar, seemingly without his consent or assistance, pulled into a steep climb and the ethereal numbers commenced their apocalyptic countdown.

5 - 4 - 3 -2 - 1 . . . . .

His thumb did not hesitate. He pushed the release button automaton like.

Commit.

The Jaguar bucked released from its burden and the invisible weapon left the pylon. He overbanked and pulled back earthwards the ground rising rapidly to meet him. He made his egress a feeling of shame washing over him.

In his rear view mirror a mushroom cloud bloomed, reminiscent of the war films he had watched as a child. Seconds later a thump rocked the airframe as the blast wave hit, shaking the jet, its passage transmitted through the controls.

Anonymous faces paraded through a dark mist, each one wearing a look of anguish. The last face was that of his sister. Her look was perplexed but accusatory. "Why?" she mouthed silently.

He bolted awake, sitting up and looking around the darkened room. All was quiet as he threw off the covers, his skin cold and clammy, his face lathered in sweat.

*

Nick started, the bright light of his alarm clock shouting the numbers. It was 0745 and he had overslept. Groaning, he kicked off the bed covers and dropped his feet to the cold linoleum tiles which covered the floor of his sparse room in the Officers' Mess. The low single storey annex was cold, the thin walls scant protection from the sharp frost which obscured the single glazed windows. He winced as his head reminded him that he had stayed well past the sensible time in the bar last night and five pints of Amstel might not have been a smart idea on a "school day". He gulped down the glass of water that had gone untouched during the night wishing he'd had the forethought to drink more before retiring to his pit.

Grabbing the dressing gown which hung on the back of the door he picked up his washing bag and made his way towards the showers. The sound of very bad singing assailed his senses as he pushed into the steamy room cursing as he realised that the three shower cubicles were already taken. All he needed. He dropped onto the slatted wooden seat nursing his head and breathing in the reviving steam. At least his rehydration process had begun. After an inordinately lengthy wait, the RAF Regiment officer emerged from a cubicle sounding disgustingly cheerful. His "ski tan" stopped at a point half way down his neck replaced by a healthy "bar tan", although his impressive physique proved that he spent quite a bit more time in the gym than his aircrew brother officer. They exchanged greetings as Nick took over, locking the rickety, slatted wooden door behind him. The rush of warm water was a welcome relief.

By the time Nick pulled on his flying suit and tied up the laces of his flying boots the clock already showed 0805 and he was now seriously behind time. Pulling on a cold weather flying jacket and his "chip bag" service hat he let himself out locking his room door behind him. All he would need for the day was in his small rucksack and he would head out to the Squadron straight after breakfast.

The dining room was packed as he served himself a bowl of cornflakes and settled into the chair at the far end of the long mahogany table. He had deliberately distanced himself from the throng of air traffic controllers who chatted noisily at the opposite end. He had no desire to share control tower stories this early in the morning. The headline in the daily rag seemed familiar and a glance at the date confirmed that it was yesterday's newspaper. Some days if the trooper flight to Decimomannu arrived early at Wildenrath the papers would be delivered on the same day. It was obviously late today and he would have to catch up later. Glancing at his watch, time was ticking away and unless he could attract attention soon he would be forgoing breakfast. A steward emerged from behind the partition which shut out the doors to the kitchen carrying a plate of delicious smelling bacon and steaming scrambled egg. His stomach responded hungrily the smell of the bacon tantalising. Who could ever be vegetarian? He tried to catch the man's eye but he disappeared back behind the partition as quickly as he had appeared.

After two more fruitless attempts Nick finally accosted the steward as he passed close by and ordered a "full fry" with all the trimmings. Nothing ambitious this morning just a straight forward order and he would be gone. Another nervous glance at his watch. He had 25 minutes to get across to Squadron Operations.

He waited and waited as more plates of food appeared and their hungry recipients wolfed them down. Eventually, Nick resigned himself to failure. Breakfast would have to wait and he would catch a slice of toast at the Squadron. He left the cheery officers to their prattling.

As he emerged into the car park the noise of the first wave split the air and he could visualise the pair of Jaguars rolling down the main runway at Brüggen in close formation. A glance at his watch verified that the pilots allocated to the dawn patrol had been more timely than his achievements this morning. Hidden behind the trees he was unable to catch sight of the jets before the noise of the engines receded, heading east into the low flying areas.

Fumbling with the car keys he poked at the icy lock willing the ice to give way more in hope than anticipation. Frozen rain was a strange phenomenon peculiar to Central Europe. The de-icer spray can taunted him from the dashboard almost mocking. It took three attempts before the ice gave way and the key was persuaded into the slot. The door cracked open and he slumped gratefully onto the cold seat. Turning the key in the ignition he was rewarded with the hesitant chatter of the starter relays signalling a flat battery. Rapid curses followed. He had been promised a Mess garage months ago by the Mess Manager but delays in postings meant that two officers had yet to move out and, meanwhile, his increasingly creaky car suffered from the damp and progressively colder mornings. No wonder it would not start. With the harsh German winter approaching he resolved to get that loan he had promised himself and buy that new Porsche 924 that everyone was raving about. There had to be some advantages of being single.

There was no choice but to take the alternative transport this morning and he pulled his trusty "Two-wheeled, Vehicular Transport Mark 1, officers for the use of...", from behind an adjacent garage. The rusty chain groaned as he persuaded the bike into action and tottered off across the car park. Overhead the leaden skies dumped more rain on the airbase deepening the air of gloom. Within minutes the cloying drizzle had soaked his cold weather flying jacket and his flying suit was clinging uncomfortably to his legs. Today just keeps on giving he thought, morosely. To make matters worse, he was now officially late.

The rain was still pelting down as he threaded his way past the barbed wire trestles at the entrance to the dispersal. At least he could park his bike next to the crewroom saving a long walk across the concrete taxiway. He hoped, desperately, that he had brought his spare flying suit back to the Squadron or he was set for a soggy morning. His "long johns", the less than attractive underwear he was required to wear when flying, clung damply to his legs heightening his misery. The bike was hoisted onto the rack joining three others in a soggy row. He wondered whether the other riders had been better prepared for the ride to work. Anyone had to have been better prepared than he was this morning he accepted ruefully.

Pushing through the door into Flying Clothing he felt the warm air radiate from the overheated refuge. He barely acknowledged the cheery greeting from the safety equipment fitter, or "squipper", as he made his way over to his locker. Dragging open the door he breathed a sigh of relief at the sight of his spare flying suit hanging on the peg. Happier now he negotiated a change of underwear with the young airman gratefully tearing open the plastic wrapping and extracting the fresh long johns. With his wet cold weather jacket now steaming over a toasty radiator life began to seem normal again.

He crossed the short distance to the "soft" accommodation quickly, anxious not to resort to his previous damp state, passing the Registry as he walked in.

"Sir, have you got a minute?" the clerk shouted as he walked by. He groaned audibly but fixed a smile to his face as he retraced his steps.

"Yes Corporal, what's the problem?"

"Two things Sir. The Boss wants to see you about the Form 540. Apparently he has a few issues with the narrative and wants some changes made."

Nick groaned. That would mean having the whole thing typed up again and he had only just got it back from the typist yesterday.

"Has he marked up the draft?" Nick asked.

"He has Sir but he wants to talk it through first. He's in with the flight commanders now but he's not flying today so you can see him when he comes out."

"OK, I'll grab a coffee first and come back for the file. Can you book it out to me?"

"I'll do that Sir. The other thing is your travel claim for your trip to the simulator has come back. Apparently they are saying that you should have used Station MT rather than your own car for the journey. They've rejected the claim."

"That's ridiculous Corporal, I started the journey from Gutersloh where I was on leave. That would have meant coming back here to Brüggen and then making a separate trip back over to the simulator at Wildenrath."

"That's as maybe Sir. You'll have to go over to Station Headquarters and argue your case or they won't pay up."

Why did administrators seem to take delight always causing problems in life? How hard could it be to have a simple travel claim paid without enduring a recurring drama? He pressed on to the crewroom, a cup of coffee and a slice of toast now high on his priority list. His stomach grumbled.

Nick arranged the fixings on the counter of the coffee bar. Butter and a tub of Nutella spread for the topping. At least his blood sugars wouldn't run low with that supplement to bolster the diet. His steaming mug of coffee would be the ideal accompaniment. He lifted the lid on the bread basket and peered in. The empty plastic bag summed his morning's lack of good luck.

CHAPTER 7

Delta Dispersal, RAF Wildenrath.

The Phantom was pushed back slowly onto the yellow marks on the floor of the hardened aircraft shelter nodding to rest as the flight line mechanic, known as "flems" or "lineys", spotted the undercarriage precisely. The roar of the tractor masked by the spooling Rolls Royce Spey jet engine subsided as the other flight line mechanic busied himself around the nosewheel unclipping the shackle and releasing the towbar. Within seconds, the tug pulled clear and the pilot signalled his intent to close down. The jet noise dwindled.

Disentangling themselves from the bulky parachute harness the crew stood up in the cockpit replacing ejection seat pins and climbing down the ladders; the cumbersome rear steps clipped over the gaping air intake, the small internal ladders dropping from the lower fuselage beneath the front cockpit.

Razor planted his feet back on terra firma clutching a strange piece of electrical cabling in this hand.

"OK I give in, what's that?" queried his bemused navigator.

"You mean you don't know?"

"It looks like the umbilical from a Sidewinder to me."

The pilot looked crestfallen.

"It's a different connector for a Sparrow. That's from the wrong missile. Looks like you've been had me old sport. I bet the armourer at Valley is laughing his socks off telling his mates that you've gone home with a bit of scrap metal thinking it's a trophy from your Sparrow firing."

"He seemed like such a good bloke too. . . . ."

"Looks like you need a few more weapons lectures to sharpen up those academic skills me old mate."

Flash emerged from the HAS angling towards the flying clothing locker room, the smile on his face hidden from his unsuspecting "stick".

*

In an adjacent HAS the harassed liney manhandled the LOX pot from the trolley wrestling with the canvas flap which covered the stored containers. The new pot was heavier than the empty one that he had just placed on the rack below and he swore as the sharp angled iron bracket thumped into his leg. He carried the green spherical container back over to the waiting Phantom. Door 16, just aft of the nosewheel leg, hung down from the underbelly, the panel latched at an angle to allow the new pot to be offered up onto the rails which would hold it securely in place in flight.

Liquid oxygen, or LOX, was literally the life blood for the crews of a combat aircraft once in the air. Above 8,000 feet, the freezing cold liquid held in the pot under pressure would turn into gaseous oxygen and provide the air which would sustain life at altitude. Deprived of this essential element the crews would quickly succumb to hypoxia, an insidious condition which if left unchecked would lead to loss of consciousness.

Armoured feed lines connected the pot to the Phantom feeding the vital element into the supply lines and onwards to the cockpits. A single electric lead registered the contents on individual gauges for each crew member. As the "liney" hooked up the lead he failed to notice that it had routed through the scissor shackle that held the door at its crazy angle. As he pushed the door back in place, the slight increase in resistance was lost on him and the "Dzus" fasteners slotted easily back into position, securing the door firmly in its housing. Inside, the crimped lead was squeezed tightly. As yet the outer shielding was unbroken but with the stresses imposed on the LOX pot under G it would eventually fail. Unintentionally, the "liney" had just set a stopwatch ticking.

CHAPTER 8

The Pilots' Briefing Facility, Alpha Dispersal, RAF Brüggen.

Nick waited patiently at the table in the Vault as the Registry Clerk shuffled through the filing cabinet looking for the correct folder. He pulled out the blood red file with "Top Secret" emblazoned across the jacket and cross-checked the reference number against his docket. Satisfied with the match he closed the cabinet once more sealing the contents away from prying eyes and from those without a "need to know". Apart from his own version of Armageddon, Nick had no need to see where his other squadron mates would be visiting should that fateful day ever dawn.

"Can I check your ID Sir," the clerk asked formally. It was a silly routine as the clerk handed classified documents to Nick on an almost daily basis but for this document it was a procedure demanded by nuclear protocols. Without his ID the document would not be released, however, temporarily. It was also ironic as Nick had prepared much of the material contained within himself. Happy that procedure had been satisfied the clerk placed the bulky folder in front of the edgy pilot and withdrew from the Vault.

Opening the folder the list of waypoints dropped onto the desk. When loaded as mission data into the tiny onboard computer in the NAVWASS, the points would make up his route to the target. The rest of the file contained maps, images and notes specific to his target, Zerbst airfield in East Germany. Pulling out the carefully folded map which would accompany him in the cockpit should he ever fly the one-way mission, he inspected it carefully. The first strip showed the route to the target, the second map showed the route back. Distinct black lines linked small circles on the map denoting turning points. The circles were annotated with two letter designations which related to pre-assigned waypoints from the war plan known as Supplan Mike. Although these would change on a daily basis, his route to Armageddon was pre-planned and other fighter bombers would route via similar waypoints on their suicide missions. A broad red line cut the route at the Inner German Border marking the transition into hostile airspace, assuming that the pre-conflict stalemate would be still in force. The likelihood was that the Soviet Forces in East Germany would already have received orders to penetrate the Border and it was anyone's guess when he would meet the first hostile forces. If intelligence estimates were to be believed, the Soviets would advance well into NATO territory during those first few hours and he would be under threat from first and second echelon forces as soon as he approached the peacetime limits of the Buffer Zone between East and West. A second line marked the point at which he would turn off his IFF transponder and, from that point on, he would be invisible to all but the primary radars of the air defence forces of the Group of Soviet Forces in Germany. He saw little solace in that thought as the range rings denoting the peacetime locations of the surface-to-air missile sites in East Germany were so dense that detection seemed inevitable. He would have to fight his way into the target area.

His Initial Point, or IP, was a bridge which lay well to the west of the town of Zerbst across the Mittelere Elbe River. His approach would be at low level flying as close to the ground as he dared. Setting off on a heading of 070 degrees at 480 knots he would run for two minutes which equated to sixteen miles at that speed before pulling up into a 60 degree climb. At the apex of the manoeuvre the weapon system would automatically release the WE 177C thermonuclear bomb into a toss trajectory and it would arc towards the target before detonating 500 feet above the technical site in a devastating airburst designed to destroy aircraft and materiel in the open.

The WE 177 was a thermonuclear weapon that used the energy from the primary nuclear fission reaction to compress and ignite a secondary nuclear fusion reaction. The result was a huge increase in explosive power compared to the earlier fission weapons. The WE 177C he was nominated to deliver weighed in at 457 kg or just over a thousand pounds so it was roughly equivalent to its conventional compatriot. With a yield of 190 kilotons, however, the destructive power it unleashed was in a different league. The safety and arming system on the weapon was inherently simple using a key operated "Strike Enable Facility"; a cylindrical barrel key, bizarrely, similar to those used on gaming machines in amusement arcades. Unique to the weapon, the key could not be used for any other purpose.

A white translucent window in the nose of the bomb housed a radar altimeter which conferred the airburst capability but a back-up ground-burst-on-impact mode was insurance against failure. A tertiary laydown capability was also available which required the delivery platform to fly overhead the target and use retarding fins on the bomb to slow its time of flight and delay the moment of impact until the fighter-bomber was clear. Leaving the Jaguar within just a short distance of the target at detonation, the latter profile was not for the faint hearted.

Once armed by the key, unlike the two man permission system used on the Phantom only a single permission was needed from the Jaguar pilot in the air during the arming sequence prior to bomb release. There were no further codes required. Once committed, the arming sequence was automatic and as electrical snatch plugs and the release lanyards disengaged, the velocity sensors deployed and the speed sensors detected a velocity greater than 120 knots, detonation was inevitable.

His mind switched back to his target but the implications weighed heavily. With the town of Zerbst lying to the West and the predominant winds blowing from the west, at least the bulk of the nuclear fallout would not drift over the town after he had delivered his weapon. The airburst was the dirtiest delivery possible. Fallout would blanket the surrounding countryside for weeks and the villages to the east would be rendered uninhabitable. Whilst some, mostly those on base, would be killed in the opening blast wave, the radiating shock wave would kill just as many. The electro-magnetic pulse would take out any unprotected electronics within a wide radius rendering communications impossible. The more sinister effect would be the radiation which would guarantee a slow insidious death from cancer over the following years.

He had little choice. If left untargeted the Mig-23 "Flogger" Regiment at Zerbst would provide fighter escort for Soviet bombers attacking his own and adjacent airfields. If he by some fluke survived the mission, they would be a constant thorn in his side for the rest of the campaign. The airfield had to be neutralised and it was his mission which would do so. It was personal.

The biggest issue was not the moral dilemma posed by his nuclear target. It was much more delicate. Nick was struggling with his sexuality. He was gay. Homosexuality was an offence under Air Force Law. Admitting to his "crime" could not be done lightly. It was not a case of "don't ask don't tell", it would mean the loss of his livelihood and the immediate rescinding of his clearances. The last person to admit to the "offence" had been summarily dismissed and only the fact that his position held no authority over others had saved him from a stretch in Colchester, the military prison.

As he had been vetted meticulously to check on his reliability to hold nuclear quick reaction alert, any suggestion that he may be vulnerable to pressure from foreign intelligence services which might lead to being compromised would, firstly, be jumped upon and, secondly, used as a reason to prevent him doing the job he loved. There were others who shared his plight but the fact was that his sexuality was illegal in the Service. He would be seen as a security risk. He could not even hint at his inner feelings to anyone on the Squadron least of all his Flight Commander or the Boss. One word and he would be grounded and an immediate investigation would begin. WRAFs were retired for becoming pregnant, so how could he expect any leniency? This one was a dilemma that could not be resolved and one that he would have to live with.

As he emerged from the vault the Duty Authoriser on the operations desk shouted over.

"Nick, OC A Flight wants to see you in his office."

"What now?" he groaned.

CHAPTER 9

The 92 Squadron Aircrew Crewroom, Delta Dispersal, RAF Wildenrath.

There was a welcoming buzz from the crewroom as Flash walked in. A group clustered around the coffee bar clutched gaudily decorated squadron mugs, names emblazoned on the side identifying each individual.

"Hail the conquering hero," a voice called out from the knot. Heads turned to greet him.

"We are not worthy," a second voice called, the banter light hearted. Arms were raised and lowered in unison, in mock salute aping a scene from a Monty Python classic episode. Flash grinned back.

"You're only jealous because you didn't get an early Christmas present too," he replied.

"How did it go?"

"Whooooooooooooshhhh," Flash responded mimicking the sound of a Sparrow express train as it left the launcher. The expletives were unrepeatable in polite circles. He made his way around to the rear of the coffee bar, loaded his own mug with a dose of instant coffee and added hot water from the recalcitrant water heater which groaned in protest.

"Piece of cake," he finally added the faces clearly expecting more detail. "It went to plan. Airborne at 0700, through the entry gate and the Jindivik was on station and ready. Absolutely text book. The missile ejected cleanly and went straight to the target. It missed the radar target and took out the Jindivik. That thing made an almighty splash as it hit the water. I've already warned Razor to expect a big Mess bill this month."

As if on cue Razor walked in, his flying suit unzipped, the arms tied around his waist in an effort to cool down. His bright yellow t-shirt with its cobra intertwined with a Phantom screamed his squadron allegiance .

"He's right on that one. The civil servants at Llanbedr were at work at 6 AM this morning. They'll be claiming a nice fat Christmas bonus with all that overtime. Must be nice. He collected the mug of coffee which Flash had pushed across the coffee bar.

The banter turned to other matters but inevitably drifted back onto flying. It was early and, unless they were lucky enough to be flying, the officers would slowly drift away as secondary duties and sundry administrative trivia beckoned. Mac McKenzie turned to his young navigator.

"Cockers, we're up for an affiliation sortie later today with our returning heroes as number two."

"I saw that Sir."

"Can you get hold of our trade and do the coordination briefing for me? I think it was 15 Squadron if I read it right."

"I do believe you're right Sir!"

"Briefing's in 20 minutes. Cut along."

Cockers left without further ado. Mac raised an eyebrow trying to decide whether the young Flying Officer was in need of a firm put down or whether his over-confidence was justified. He exchanged a knowing look with Flash. If so, he had best perform well in the air today or he may find the rest of his convex a tad more challenging.

CHAPTER 10

Alpha Dispersal, RAF Brüggen.

The Officer Commanding A Flight, or OCA to the squadron, grimaced at the closely typed draft in the file in front of him. Nick stood firmly to attention in front of him.

"This is just not good enough Nick. You've done ISS for goodness sake. A schoolboy with a grade C "O" Level could have done better than this. This is the official operations record for the Squadron for Pete's sake. Historians will read this in the future and take this as gospel. It's not even accurate."

The tirade went on and Nick stood stiffly not yet sure if this was a hats-on interview or not.

"Sit down for goodness sake. Look. I've made some corrections. The dates for the trappers visit were wrong and the two jets that landed at Jever were working with the F-104 squadron up there, not with the Phantoms. The Phantoms are based at Wittmundhafen. There are a bunch of other changes needed to turn it into some semblance of the English language. Get it retyped and I want to see it again before it goes to the Boss for signature. Any questions, speak to me later this morning before I go flying. I want it on my desk when I get back down on the ground."

"Yes Sir, my apologies I'll get it sorted straight away."

“Anyway enough of that, are you ready for your sortie? Run through the profile for me now and I’ll authorise it.”

Nick outlined his mission plan as his flight commander listened, keen to find fault.

“OK that met report sounds optimistic to me. Double check with the met man before you walk and, if in doubt, fly the altex in the westerly low flying area. I’ll put you in the sheets for a practice QRA profile. TWOATAF SOPs, low flying not below 250 feet MSD. Don’t forget you’re carrying a “shape” so no reaction if bounced. Waggle off any attacks. You’re down for a toss profile against your practice target near Gütersloh. That about covers it. Any questions?"

“No Sir, I’m happy with that.”

“OK the authoriser tells me you have Alpha Delta in HAS 27. Get off at 1330 Zulu and I’ll authorise you for 1 hour 45 minutes. Use an operational mission callsign. You’ll be Four Alpha Tango Echo.”

Nick rose to leave.

“Oh, and Nick.” A pause.

“I’ve just had HQ P&SS on the phone. Your security vetting has been brought forward. The investigator wants to see you next Tuesday does that fit?”

“Yes Sir,” he said quietly. His heart sank. There was no putting it off now.

Nick left the office smarting and promptly locked the Secret file in his desk drawer in the aircrew office. It would have to wait or his planning for the trip would not get done. He would be on a short fuse this afternoon once his trip was done. He did not fancy incurring his flight commander’s wrath a second time in one day. The ops room beckoned.

CHAPTER 11

The 92 Squadron Operations Room, RAF Wildenrath.

Cockers glanced at his watch as he drew a copy of the briefing proforma from the slot on the front of the ops desk. The content was becoming familiar and, despite his relative inexperience, he was increasingly happy with the routine. Filling out the simple form would allow them to increase the defensive reaction the "targets" were allowed from a simple 90 degree turn to two full 360 degree turns with a reversal in heading. From a simple sighting exercise, it would become, tactically, much more interesting with the opponents fighting back.

Glancing at the board he took in the details of the sortie; Buccaneers from 15 Squadron at Laarbruch were today's opponents and tough opposition they would be too. It should be a fun sortie. The sortie had already been allocated a pair of Phantoms by the Duty Authoriser and a quick check in the radar diary showed a pair of good radars. The omens were good. Possession of the aircraft was half the battle and he felt sorry for the sortie below theirs which had yet to be allocated airframes. The chances of a serviceable Phantom being available as the day wore on lessened with time.

He leafed through the briefing folder jotting down the telephone number for the operations desk at Laarbruch. Adding the mission call signs from the ops board he made a few routine annotations such as the minimum heights and maximum speeds. He would love to alter these parameters to add a little spice but the Air Staff rules gave little latitude. Staff officers at

HQ RAF Germany seemed to have little sense of humour when charges of low level hooliganism were bandied around.

He picked up the handset and dialled. A few short rings later a familiar voice answered the call:

“15 Squadron, Flight Lieutenant Gilbert.”

It was his old friend from training days at Finningley. They had suffered together the stresses and strains of being taught to navigate using the stars in the darkened rear cabin of a Dominie training jet. Both had moved on to fast jets where they could see out of the window and he was eternally grateful for the escape.

“Gilbers old chap, it’s Cockers down on 92. How are you doing?”

"Cockers me old mate, I’m great. Are we working with you today?”

“You are old son. The premier fighter squadron is out for your ass. Hope you’re feeling sharp.”

“In your dreams. You can keep that big old radar wagging away but you’ll never see us again.”

The banter was traditional and harmless and expected between crews on the squadrons.

“Are you leading the sortie?”

“Not quite me old, I’m just the secretary. The QWI is leading. Do you know Mac McKenzie? A good bloke.”

“Yes I met him at a beer call last month. A good guy for an air defender.”

"He is until he starts asking difficult questions about rockets! I lose track after about thirty seconds when he gets onto seeker head theory.”

“Tell me about it. Our weapons leader is just the same. I’m sure he builds laser guidance heads in his basement at home. Seriously weird if you ask me. Anyway, have you got some details for me? Where are you planning to operate? Our plan was to take a look at the weather over in Area 3 and then to work around past Gütersloh and come back from the north. Does that work?

"We can cover that. Our met man is saying that Area 3 will be out of limits for us so we'll stick to Area 2. We can tap you on the way back down. How far north are you heading?"

"We have a laydown attack planned for Nordhorn Range and then we'll route past Hopsten into the area around Coesfeld. We should be there at 1344 Zulu."

"That sounds good. I think there's a formation of F-104s heading south about the same time and we may have a go against them too. We'll deconflict the timings and we should be able to tap both of you."

"Outstanding, let's just run through the proforma and that'll make it legal. OK we're Anvil formation, two Buccaneers. . . . ."

Each detail was carefully noted ready to form the core of the mission briefing in a few minutes time.

CHAPTER 12

Alpha Dispersal, RAF Brüggen.

Nick walked out of the ops room and crossed the short distance to the flying clothing locker room. It was good to escape the confines of the hardened bunker and feel some fresh air filling his lungs. The morning had been a litany of failures and the frustration at his inability to control events was beginning to tell. He had to clear his mind for the impending mission. Getting airborne in this frame of mind was never a good idea but the last thing he was going to admit to his flight commander was that he wasn't fit to fly. That would have been tantamount to admitting to LMF; lack of moral fibre. It may be an outdated concept but machismo was alive and well on this Squadron.

He pushed open the door and exchanged a brief greeting with the "squipper" as he made his way over to his locker to collect his flying kit. A trio of pilots swapped banter as they dumped their life jackets and helmets onto the green, baize-covered table at the front of the locker room, the post-sortie adrenaline barely dissipated. Their happy camaraderie grated. Trying to focus on the task to come he avoided contact skirting around the densely packed aisle towards his own locker. Dragging open the door he pulled out his external G suit drawing it around his waist and zipping up the sides of the ungainly assembly pulling it snugly around his legs. Donning his damp cold weather jacket for protection against the cold winter weather he slid the life jacket over the top, clipping the breast plates together tight around his chest. Collecting his helmet he made a swift exit before his squadron mates could engage him in trivial repartee. Had he done a quick helmet check on the test set before leaving he might have saved further grief.

The cold air whipped around his head as he dragged on his bonedome as he walked across the taxiway towards HAS 27 and his waiting jet. The lack of activity should have been his first warning.

It was HAS 27 wasn't it? He should have concentrated more at the out brief but he assumed that OCA had been correct when he had authorised the sortie. Which jet he had been allocated was fairly important. Whatever the problem there could be no doubting that he was at the wrong HAS. The doors were closed and the familiar drone of the Houchin external power set was blatantly absent. He trudged back towards operations cursing silently.

Approaching HAS 24 he saw the familiar bustle as the "lineys" made preparations for the see-off. The external power was hooked up, headphones plugged in and chocks positioned under the main wheels. This was more in keeping with how it should be. Progress!

He signed for the jet in the management cabin his helmet still plugged firmly on his head and climbed up the ladder to the cockpit unaware of the knowing glances from the groundcrew below. "Bloody pilots," the liney mouthed to his mate with a roll of the eyes.

Nick dropped onto the seat having given his ejection seat a cursory check and fiddled with the array of straps disentangling himself prior to strapping in. He plugged his PEC into the slot on the seat expecting the reassuring hum of the intercom but all was quiet in his earphones. He unplugged the PEC and re-seated it into the housing on the ejection seat and was rewarded with the expected noise. Just a connection problem he thought as he fired up the radio box, the chatter from Squadron Operations filling his headset. He waited a moment before thumbing the transmit button on the throttles for a radio check. Nothing. He reselected the microphone switch on the front of his oxygen mask but still his words were muted in his padded cocoon. Gesturing to the Man A he beckoned the liney up the ladders pointing animatedly at his oxygen mask giving the universal thumbs down. He disappeared, reappearing across the HAS en route to the management cabin to summon the safety equipment worker. Nick busied himself with the rest of his checks as he waited for the technician to appear.

It had been five minutes since the telephone call had been made but still no sign of the safety equipment specialist. He tapped, frustratedly, on the cockpit sill as he watched through the open front doors. Eventually he appeared, ambling gently across the taxiway towards the waiting Jaguar. Nick made an urgent hurry along with his hands which elicited precisely zero response from the indifferent tradesman. Clearly Nick's priorities and his differed somewhat. He'd have a word when he got back after the sortie.

A head finally appeared above the cockpit sill and the squipper placed the spare mask on the edge of the cockpit grasping the lip to steady himself. Nick had already detached the unserviceable mask and thrust it aside grasping the proffered replacement. The mask clipped quickly onto the chain harness on the helmet held in place by a fiddly red grommet. Nick, clad in leather flying gloves happily delegated the awkward task to the technician. The bulky connector attaching the microphone lead to the housing was pushed into place perhaps a little over enthusiastically and the heavy pressure rattled his head inside the padded helmet. Was the assistance just slightly over zealous? By now that was of no consequence and he flipped over the microphone switch thankfully hearing the sound of his own dulcet tones in his bonedome.

"Diamond, Four Alpha Tango Echo, radio check."

" Four Alpha Tango Echo, this is Diamond, loud and clear."

He was back on track but his day really couldn't get any better.

CHAPTER 13

The 92 Squadron Briefing Room, RAF Wildenrath.

"Gents the met."

Mac picked up the spidery graphic and held it in full view of the aircrew arranged along the front seats in the compact briefing room.

"A warm front passed through here at 1000 Zulu and now lies overhead Gütersloh. It cleared through Cologne/Bonn at 1045 and lies somewhere to the east right now. The front slowed as it encountered the Harz Mountains and the precise timing is keeping the met man guessing but he expects a slow improvement during the next few hours. Conditions are improving at this end of Low Flying Area 3 but it's presently unfit for our purposes with cloud on the hills and no gaps in the cloud deck. We could operate below - just - but if we had to pull up there's no way back down through it. Conditions should be better out there later in the day but for now it's Low Fly 2 for us. Weather behind the front is good with unlimited vis. Yes I know, I said unlimited visibility and no significant cloud. That's an unusual phenomena on the North German Plain so don't get too used to it!"

The graphic returned to its slot on the overhead projector stand ready for the next crews.

"Let's get into the meat of the sortie and then Cockers will cover the trade that's planned for today. The good news is that, as well as the Buccaneers, we've had a call from the F-104 outfit at Jever who want to play."

The OHP flicked on bathing the room in a bright light. The familiar sound of a Zippo lighter presaged a wisp of smoke as Cockers lit up a Marlboro cigarette.

"The domestics. We are callsigns Mike Lima 66 and 72, Whiskey and Romeo in HASs 47 and 54. Both are Charlie fit with a gun and carrying an acquisition Sidewinder. The number 1 diversion is Hopsten with 4,200 lbs on the ground and the crash diversion is Brüggen. We're visual recoveries with 2,800 lbs on the ground. We'll go for individual checks and call ready to taxy on Stud 10 at 1255 to be airborne on the hour. Line up as a pair for a pairs takeoff and a "playtex" into battle formation at 350 knots. We'll carry out a standard low level departure for Area 2 transiting at 500 feet and 350 knots. No reaction to any threats until we're in the low flying area but as soon as we cross the Rhine, complete your weapons checks and the game's on. Fuel calls; give me a Bingo 1 when the external tanks are empty and a Bingo 2 at 6,000 lbs. Run your own chicken fuel but call me if you get that low and we'll come back as a pair. The weather's good so we'll do a pairs recovery from a low level north arrival for a visual run-in-and-break from battle formation. If you have fuel to spare finish up with a few circuits for practice."

To a layman the gabbled information would have been unintelligible but to the crews it was the vital information which would set the scope of the sortie. With the information recorded it would set a series of flags throughout the mission which would ensure its safe execution.

A quiet word from the Duty Authoriser before he had entered the briefing room had raised Mac's eyebrows but he was about to impart the good news.

"We have an additional task today that looks like it'll be quite good fun. It's our chance to wake up the Commies who just happened to be camped out on the base perimeter at the Nike site at Kempen. They think that they're being nice and secretive and have holed up in a ditch close to the access road but an eagle eyed guard spotted them and called them in. The counter-intelligence team plan to round them up and see them on their way but they've asked us to fly a show of presence first to wake them up. We'll pay them a visit on the transit outbound and if we have the gas, we'll also say hello on the way home. We can't have the Soviet spies from SOXMIS thinking they have unfettered access to our secrets can we?"

He dragged out a dog eared low flying map that had, probably, served Pontius when he was a pilot.

"This is our normal route which passes right overhead where they are camped out. We'll go through the overhead and carry out a left hand orbit to reattack from the south on the second pass. We'll clip the Laarbruch MATZ in the turn so we'll give Laarbruch Approach a call as we head north to clear our movements. They're expecting us and I hear a couple of Jaguar recce. birds have already said good morning on the way out. Razor, stick with me in the turn and stay in fighting wing for the pass, OK?"

He received an answering nod.

"OK, Cockers, run through the affiliation briefing and finish up with any points you want to add about the tactical procedures. If it's SOP then that works for me."

Cockers stood up and began to read the details from his briefing sheet. Flash scribbled furiously on his kneeboard capturing the key tactical information.

Briefing over, the crews emerged from the briefing room and clustered around the operations desk. Mac entered the details into the authorisation sheets and initialled the authorisation column for both jets approving the detail.

The Duty Authoriser scanned the planning board for final details before turning back to his checklist for the "Out Briefing".

"OK gents, you have aircraft Whiskey, Mike Lima 66 and Romeo, Mike Lima 72 in HASs 47 and 54 respectively. You've had the met brief. The front is about here," he gestured pointing to a position to the east of Cologne. "Gutersloh is still red so it's not through there yet but a PIREP from a jet in Area 3 said it's clear over the Möhne See. Expect the weather to pick up soon. Your area here," he said moving his hand across to the Dutch border to the north of Laarbruch, "is good so expect good flying conditions en route and in the area. No change in the diversions and the flying state is still visual recoveries with crash fuel on the ground. You're in the sheets for TWOATAF SOPs as briefed working with Anvil and Baron formations, minimum heights are 500 feet en route and 250 feet in the area. Cockers has briefed the rules of engagement. The jets are ready and your see-off crews are at the HASs. Clear to walk."

The crews dispersed making their way to the flying clothing locker rooms for their flying kit.

"Chief; walking for Whiskey and Romeo," the Duty Authoriser called to the engineering controller in the next room.

"OK Sir, the see-off crews are at the shelters now."

*

Mac began his usual circuit of the jet, part of the normal acceptance. At each stage he checked items off a mental check list. As he had learned to fly the Phantom at the Operational Conversion Unit he had clutched his flight reference cards in hand ticking off each check in turn. This procedure had long since been committed to memory and he systematically checked the airframe for damage, that panels were secure, that the undercarriage oleos were correctly extended and that the tyres and brake lines had no wear or damage. Dotted around the airframe were tiny gauges and the correct pressure for each one was registered in his memory. Each passed the test. As he rounded the huge afterburner cans at the rear of the engines he stretched up and pulled the tell tale from the housing at the rear of the aircraft arming the brake parachute. He peered into the cavernous exhaust checking the massive rings that fed fuel into the jet pipes giving the enormous increase in thrust which the Phantom needed in order to manoeuvre. As he reached the inner weapons pylon on the port side he did a double take. When he had signed for the jet, the Form 700 had recorded a Sidewinder acquisition round fitted to the LAU-7 missile launcher on the port outer station. The LAU was there but the missile was distinctly absent. He called the liney over.

"You may have spotted the deliberate error but there's no acqui. round."

"I thought it was odd Sir. I'll get the armourers over right away and get one fitted."

"The loading certificate was signed up and coordinated Chief. Someone's cocked up big time."

The crew chief looked appropriately embarrassed. Someone would be looking at a week's jankers for this one. Mac clambered the steps set into the forward fuselage and dropped into the cockpit. Cockers had already applied external power, the instruments were humming and the lights blazing as he checked his Martin Baker ejection seat; his ultimate insurance policy. Beginning his left-to-right checks, by the time he had scanned around the cockpit, the armourer was dragging a missile trolley in through the front doors of the HAS, the sleek acquisition round strapped onboard. He would sit tight. There was little that could go wrong with the simple process of slotting the round onto the launcher - or so he hoped. He also hoped the armourers had been more diligent with preparing his ejection seat.

In the tightly packed bay underneath the Phantom, the LOX pot hissed its contents into the oxygen feed lines. In the cockpits the gauge showed almost full. It would only be the rigours of the upcoming low level mission that would highlight the procedural glitch.

Finally ready, Mac circled his fist, a finger raised, receiving a thumbs up from the liney as the first of the Spey engines wound up. He slotted into a familiar routine watching the RPMs rise and checking temperatures and pressures as the engine rumbled into life. A series of checks ensued to ensure that each of the myriad of aircraft systems was operating normally and would power the essential services that the Phantom would need during the upcoming mission.

The liney unclipped his headset and emerged into the bright sunlight adjusting his ear defenders against the shriek of the jet engines. He turned to face the belligerent Phantom checking the clearance on the wingtips subconsciously. The other flight line mechanic moved across towards the rear of the main wheels and on a signal from the cockpit, pulled the chocks from beneath the wheels releasing the straining jet . With the dayglo bats above his head he rechecked the clearance before waving the pilot clear of the HAS, the Phantom nodding briefly as the brake check temporarily arrested its progress. Moving to the side the liney signalled ahead and the Phantom rolled by, it's jet engines quietening as it followed the centreline marking towards the taxiway.

The pair of Phantoms emerged from the trees which ringed the loop taxiway and Mac checked them in on the Tower frequency. Ahead, their progress was ominously blocked by an immovable object. The bulk of a hemp coloured Nimrod straddled the taxiway its four engines spooling away, the flattened grass alongside the concrete marking the jet efflux. The frequency was quiet but that was not the reason for Mac's unease. The markings on the fin, a red goose, denoted the insignia of the Squadron tasked with electronic intelligence duties. Based at Wyton in the United Kingdom, the Nimrods crossed the world, the crews in the darkened rear cabin listening intently to radio frequencies and recording electronic emissions to work out the intentions of potential foes. Their activity was covert and compromising a discreet launch and the procedures which surrounded it in order to maintain radio silence, would attract unwanted interviews with strange men. Mac knew that to announce the presence of the aircraft ahead would be to compromise its mission, almost certainly a covert run along the Inner German Border. He drew the Phantom to a halt and waited.

Eventually, without a word over the radio, the Nimrod pulled onto the runway. Its four engines spooled up and it trundled off down the runway lifting off into the bright skies and heading east climbing gently. It was as if it had never existed.

Mac glanced at the clock conscious that they were now pressed for time. The other Phantom crossed through his mirrors and lined up in close echelon on his wing. The pilot's head disappeared inside the cockpit engrossed in his instruments. Mac eased up the throttles and the noise in the cockpit rose to match his actions. The airframe shook slightly as it strained against the brakes. The engine instruments stabilised and he checked the temperatures in turn. The left was steady at the placard limits but the right was worryingly high. He warned Cockers before hitting the transmit button.

"Tower Mike Lima 66 has an engine problem. Request clearance onto the ORP and can you have my operators send an engine man out?"

"Mike Lima 66 roger. Cleared back to the ORP and call in position. Speaking to your operators now."

Mac eased forward giving his wingman some leeway before swinging around on the runway. The two Phantoms crossed head to head as the wingman followed his lead. Back on the taxiway he swung around in a big arc lining up on the ORP clear of the taxiway. He tapped his fingers irritably on the coaming as he waited for the engine fitter to arrive.

As he waited, a pair of 19 Squadron Phantoms taxied past, lined up and rolled off down the runway without drama. It merely added to the frustration.

After what seemed like an age, a drab green Land Rover screeched to a halt alongside and a technician clad in grey overalls topped by a camouflaged foul weather jacket climbed out, his ear defenders clamped in place over his head. Disappearing beneath the jet there was a pause before a voice piped up over the intercom.

"You're supposed to be airborne Sir, what's the problem?"

"Tell me about it. The right engine's running hot during the run-up check on the runway. Has this jet had any history of engine problems?"

"No Sir, not this one. We've had trouble with one of the other jets with a slow reheat light but no snags on Whiskey for quite a time. What temperature is it hitting?"

"It peaked at about 680 briefly but dropped back down again. It was only out of limits momentarily but I thought I'd check. Better safe than sorry."

"I'd suggest another run-up now and see how it behaves. If it's back to normal you could take it and monitor it during the sortie. If it shows any signs in the air bring it straight back and we'll do some static runs. Do you want to try it now?"

"Yes I'll give it another shot, stand by."

"Tower Mike Lima 66 am I clear for an engine run on the ORP?"

"Mike Lima 66, Wildenrath Tower affirmative. Clear run up in your present position, call me complete."

"Mike Lima 66."

He signalled to the engine fitter and spooled up the errant right hand engine. It wound up smoothly to 100% on the RPM gauge and the temperature stabilised within normal limits at 650 degrees Centigrade. Two further cycles produced the same result.

"Looks like it's cleared," he announced to the expectant technician below. "I'm happy with that and I'll watch it in the air."

"OK Sir. We'll pull it on landing and see if we can reproduce it on the ground. It might just be a glitch on the engine control amplifier. See you back in dispersal after the sortie."

The technician would never be called upon to carry out the rectification work. Events were moving inexorably towards a pre-destined conclusion.

"Tower, Mike Lima 66, 72 takeoff."

*

Before reaching their designated low flying area the Phantom crews faced a complex low level departure from RAF Wildenrath through the congested airspace around the airfield. Sitting just inside West German territory RAF Wildenrath lay just a few miles from the boundary with Dutch airspace which began only five miles to the west. With predominantly westerly winds, Phantoms departing from Runway 27 turned tightly to the south to remain over Germany, descending to 500 feet remaining in the Wildenrath circuit to avoid spreading an incessant diet of jet noise, although for those who lived under the circuit pattern it was an unavoidable curse.

The standard departure began on an easterly heading to an initial turning point close to the local town of Erkelenz before turning north to cross the first major navigation feature, the communications tower which dominated the skyline over the Joint Headquarters at RAF Rheindahlen. As they passed over the military base the Phantoms bracketed the tower, careful to maintain 500 feet above ground level. It was a point of principle amongst the crews to register their presence to the administrators at the

Headquarters who enjoyed late starts and leisurely lunches. Equally, spread amongst the "ground pounders" was a smattering of aircrew both British and NATO who would easily recognise a jet flying below its authorised height. Marking a presence was fine but securing a low flying complaint was careless.

A few miles further north the formation crossed the extended centreline of RAF Brüggen as a Jaguar made a leisurely radar approach to the main runway. Only a few miles from touchdown the approaching aircraft was a mere 500 feet above the high speed jets as they threaded their way through the crowded departure lane. The northerly leg skirted the edge of the control zone surrounding Düsseldorf International Airport just to the east keeping the crews busy consulting low flying maps ensuring, diligently, that they avoided controlled airspace. The Phantoms' flight paths crossed as they reefed into a cross turn overhead the Nike surface-to-air missile site located near the village of Kempen. Turning through the overhead, the site was a visible demonstration that the Cold War could go hot at any time. Missile crews held a permanent vigil, their deadly weapons mounted on the launch rails ready to be used in anger. The presently dormant missiles were only a few switch selections away from instant readiness. Continuing north-easterly still skirting controlled airspace, the fighters passed overhead the small town of Kamp-Lintfort, crossing the extended centreline of the Laarbruch military air traffic zone. It was here that they would complete their first task of the day.

"Laarbruch Approach Mike Lima 66, 72."

"Mike Lima 66, 72 Laarbruch Approach, loud and clear how me?"

"Loud and clear also. Two Phantoms overhead Kamp Lintfort in a left hand orbit standing by for instructions."

"Mike Lima 66, 72 squawk 3641 with ident."

"Squawking, Mike Lima 66, 72."

With a simple selection on the IFF box, the lead aircraft was now transmitting an identification signal to the secondary surveillance radar equipment in the nearby control room at Laarbruch. Unique to the controller, the code signified that he had just taken control of the orbiting jets. Given the nature of the planned exercise that might be useful insurance cover for the crews.

"Mike Lima 66, 72 standby for Talon 21 on this frequency."

The transmission from the forward air controller sounded tinny and distant in comparison to the rich tones of the radar controller closeted in his snug control room. That the transmissions emanated from a camouflaged scrape in a field some miles to the west was a detail lost on the Phantom crews in the cockpits. The British special forces operative monitoring the Soviet team had been holed up alone and unsupported for the last 24 hours, his vigil constant, his scrutiny unremitting. He trained his binoculars on his target, a pair of camouflaged bodies lying prone alongside the missile site, their binoculars trained in turn on the Nike tracking radar. The long lens of the camera was invisible to him but the small directional antenna which had been trained on the installation was clearly evident above the hedgerow. Their electronic eavesdropping was about to be rudely interrupted.

"Mike Lima 66, confirm your approach heading will be from the south?"

"Affirmative 66 repositioning now. We'll run from south to north through the overhead."

"Are you contact with the missile site?"

"Affirmative, contact."

"Roger your target is 200 yards south west of the site entrance to the west of the access road. Target is two persons; stationary. Make your pass down the line of the road, 50 yards to the east at 250 feet. Request high speed pass."

The Phantom crews were delighted to oblige.

"Mike Lima 72, fighting wing go."

Razor and Flash in the second Phantom dropped into loose formation on Mac's wing as the pair reversed their course entering a wide left hand orbit. Normally precluded from penetrating the military air traffic zone around Laarbruch, the fact that they were under positive control gave them the authority to penetrate so they took a wide berth on the Nike site remaining unseen from the ground. Positioning for the pass, Mac could see the road leading into the main gate precisely as the forward air controller had described. He marked off the distance to where he thought the Soviet agents would be, mentally noting the small intersection in the road. There!

"Confirm my target is at the road intersection?"

"Affirmative, 20 yards east of the junction."

"Contact."

The Phantoms continued the wide arc bisecting the runway centreline as they positioned for the pass. Mac eased the jet down in the turn, the turbulence buffeting the airframe. Strictly speaking they were not in the low flying area so he should have been holding a minimum height of 500 feet but the man had asked nicely and it was rude not to say good morning properly to the Soviet Liaison Team, patiently monitoring the radar emissions at the Nike site. The radio altimeter burbled its warning as it registered a height somewhat lower than the 200 foot bug that Mac had set.

Lining up on the road as he had been briefed Mac registered a black VW Passat briefly in his peripheral vision its passage registering as it flashed past along the road. As he approached the intersection he lit the afterburners and the Speys responded with a muted thump as tons of aviation fuel ignited in the burner cans at the aft of the airframe. He dropped the left wing confirming that he had passed directly overhead the intersection before reversing the turn to realign himself alongside the road. The radio altimeter complained once more. The bulk of the target tracking radar stood tall above the fields and he vaguely registered a sea of faces standing alongside. The operators had clearly been forewarned of the spectacle. All that was missing to make it seem like a spectator sport were the obligatory score boards.

"Mike Lima 66, 72 are clear and climbing."

"Roger 66, 72," came the tinny response almost drowned out with the roar of jet noise. "Do you have fuel for a second pass from north to south?"

It was churlish to refuse and, as they had to return back north to continue into the low flying area, he may as well fit in a third pass whilst he was at it.

“Affirmative, 66,72 repositioning. Cross turn go!”

The Phantoms pulled back around rapidly dropping back to low level and retracing their flight path. The second pass was even more spectacular.

“Mike Lima 66, 72 thanks for the help," came the voice of the air traffic controller. "That looked perfect for our needs and thanks. Squawk 4321 and cleared to en route. Enjoy the rest of your sortie.”

“Squawking 4321 and back to tactical. Mike Lima 66, 72. Enjoyed it Sir and thanks for the opportunity. Mike Lima 66, 72, TAD 423, TAD 423, go!”

With the ad hoc exercise complete they pressed on towards the entry point at Wesel on the mighty Rhine river. An industrial complex, “the POL” guarded the doorway to the low flying area. Pronounced “pee oh ell”, the factory on the River Rhine with its large chimneys was a significant visual navigation feature both entering and leaving the area. Dominated by a large mast standing over 260 feet above ground level it offered a welcome cue, particularly in poor weather conditions.

Heading northwards, now over the river and in the low flying area beyond, the “fight was on”.

The southerly of the two low flying areas which encompassed the North German Plain, Low Flying Area 2 was a firm favourite with the crews from Wildenrath extending from the River Rhine in the south as far as the Hopsten military air traffic zone in the north and from the Dutch border in the west to the town of Münster in the east. Although relatively narrow at the southern end and bounded by the cities of the Ruhr, the area widened to the north giving comparatively free airspace in which to engage a low flying opponent. The major disadvantage was that the two large towns of Coesfeld and Borken lay in the centre of the area and, with restrictions on overflight at low level, provided a constant irritant to the crews lying right at the point where a typical intercept would occur. Invariably as the tactical approach to the target reached its climax, pilots would see one of the towns between them and the target requiring an evasive manoeuvre to avoid overflight. Having to avoid a town at a critical moment in an engagement might dictate the success or otherwise of an intercept. Passing directly overhead would incur the wrath of an increasingly intolerant German population. A mast near the village of Osterwick stood tall above the landscape offering an excellent datum to anchor the combat air patrol as it could be seen easily from miles around with its bright red and white markings and prominent lights. After a melee, the bright markings and broad vertical extent offered an easy rendezvous point at which to regroup.

Being flat and relatively close to Wildenrath, the area was a good compromise offering a short transit flight and giving the longest time on task before fuel was exhausted and recovery was inevitable. With natural choke points at each end, the low flying area funnelled NATO aircraft routing southerly towards the Clutch airfields, the German base at Nörvenich and FOURATAF airspace beyond ensuring that any lurking Phantoms would find a "target rich environment".

Further to the north, Low Flying Area 1 in northern Germany extended from Hopsten in the south to Oldenburg in the north and from the Dutch border in the west to Bremen in the east. Although the low flying area only extended for about 50 miles east/west, there was a further area of clear airspace beyond the boundary with a minimum height of 500 feet extending the potential operating area. There were two principal radar combat air patrols, or RCAPs, in Low Flying Area 1, the first of which was the village of Herzlake to the south-west of the area orientated to the east. This detected traffic emerging from the Gütersloh area, most of which headed westwards towards Nordhorn Range which sat in the extreme west of the low flying area. A second RCAP located at the Peheim mast and orientated north-south would cover traffic heading from the low flying areas to the south towards the northern German bases of Wittmundhafen and Jever. The landscape in the area was typical of the North German Plain; absolutely flat which made the airspace ideal for unfettered low level evasion exercises. There were no gulleys in which ground attack crews could hide which meant that detection was guaranteed and the terrain was predictable. It was an ideal training ground for new crews learning the art of low level air combat. It also meant that in marginal weather which was common, there was less chance of flying into a hillside which could be an annoyance! Providing crews took careful note of the location of the obstacles, such as masts, they could operate in conditions which might otherwise seem impossible, even in the most marginal weather.

To the south-western corner of Low Flying Area 1 was one of the most significant landmarks in northern Germany. A large power station known as "Smokey Joe's" sat in a gap in the Osnabrück Ridge between the Hopsten military air traffic zone and Nordhorn Range. Visible for miles around over the flat landscape, it provided a welcome reference for many a hard-pressed aviator who may have been manoeuvring hard and become "temporarily unsure of his position". It also provided a nice lead-in feature which meant that aircraft transiting between Low Flying Areas 1 and 2 would be unlikely to penetrate controlled airspace.

Today, Low Flying Area 2 would be the Phantom's operating area.

With the intelligence detail complete and once more operating autonomously, the Phantoms emerged into the area to set up their combat air patrol. Flown as a pair their datum was positioned at the end of the inbound leg. On the outbound leg, or "hot" leg, looking in the direction from where the threat was expected to emerge, the radars would scan for inbound threats. Normally two minutes long flown at 420 knots covering a distance of 14 miles, at the end of each leg a cross turn was flown in which each Phantom turned hard towards each other at 3G, levelling up momentarily at the 90 degree point for a "belly check", before completing the turn. Most turns were flown radio silent and the wingman would initiate the turn at the appropriate point. If the wingman was having a bad day or the leader wished to return to CAP early, a violent wing waggle would prompt a turn back. The CAP was flown at 1,500 feet above ground level, firstly to remain clear of the light aircraft band above but also to give the best compromise with radar detection. At that height the radar horizon was about 27 miles which meant that there was limited time to complete any complicated geometry during an intercept. The AN/AWG 12 radar would normally show the target as soon as it popped over the horizon.

With the prominent mast at Osterwick growing in the windscreen the two Phantoms climbed gently up from low level to their patrol height.

CHAPTER 14

Hardened Aircraft Shelter 24, RAF Brüggen.

As the canopy firmly closed with the familiar thunk meeting the unyielding seals, the latches dropping into place, and Nick breathed a sigh of relief. He felt the familiar pressure on his ear drums as the cabin pressurisation kicked in and warm demisting air flowed over the cockpit coaming. The temperature in the cockpit thawed, the dials of the instruments before him giving off an artificial glow and an illusion of security. Familiarity and wellbeing replaced anxiety, blowing away the sense of frustration that had been growing since his alarm clock had signalled the start of the day. Things would improve now; or so he hoped.

Nick finished his pre take off checks and he canted the jet across the taxiway at the holding point for Runway 27. He snapped the taxilight off signalling to the runway controller in the caravan that he was ready for takeoff. He had yet to make his radio call.

Airmanship told him that he should check that the approach was clear before lining up but his intuition failed him yet again. He moved the throttles forward and the Jaguar began to move forward its pace quickening as the thrust from the Adour jet engines overcame the inertia. He kicked the rudder pedals around lining up with the prominent centreline marker on the taxiway and crossed the line marking the marshalling point.

The transmission split the calm.

“Ascot 3462 overshoot, I say again overshoot, acknowledge.”

“Overshooting, Ascot 3462.”

The sky suddenly darkened in Nick’s cockpit as the bulk of the Andover transport aircraft lumbered back into the air its undercarriage already retracting into the wheel wells. It had just finished its calibration run checking the accuracy of the instrument landing system. Whether it had been cleared to land, to roll or to overshoot was moot. Nick's stomach lurched as he recognised the enormity of his mistake. But for the sharp eyes of the local controller the huge Andover might have landed on top of him, crushing the Jaguar, destroying both aircraft and almost certainly ending Nick’s life. It had been a potentially fatal mistake and one which would return to haunt him.

“Four Alpha Tango Echo you are **now** cleared for takeoff, surface wind is 080 at ten knots.”

The rebuke was implicit.

As he finally departed the circuit, the main runway at Brüggen receding in his mirrors, Nick willed himself to relax. He was back in his element, alone in the cockpit and isolated from his errors. As he swung around onto south the tiny bug in the centre of the projected map display on his NAVWASS followed the turn. It tracked his progress as he made his way along the boundary of the Cologne/Bonn control zone. The suburbs stretched away to the east and, on the horizon, the twin spires of Cologne Cathedral stood tall. The wide expanse of the mighty Rhine flanked his passage on the left and he looked ahead to identify his next turning point, an industrial complex west of the town of Pulheim. Flying directly overhead he turned back north easterly to cross the river holding a steady 500 feet above the ground. The industrial complex of the Ruhr spread out around him as his track threaded through the suburbs between the vast cities of Cologne and Bonn. To his right airliners descended into the traffic pattern for Bonn International, flying obediently in trail as they sought out the runway to deposit their passengers back on terra firma.

The winter sun was lowering in the sky behind him even at this early hour in the afternoon. It cast a bright glow across the countryside prompting him to drop his dark visor to shade his eyes. Reflections highlighted small particles of debris and flies dotting the windscreen already even though he had barely been airborne for a few minutes, reducing his forward vision. Ahead the small town of Solingen acted as a lead-in feature for the Wüpperfurth lakes, his next turning point. Once clear of the lakes the low flying area opened out and he could drop down to 250 feet above the ground.

Heading south easterly past the control and reporting centre at Erndtebrück, his airspeed pegged at 420 knots, a lone German Phantom its camouflaged bulk dark against the horizon, passed through his extended centreline well above his height. A sudden flash of the distinctive planform signalled his detection and the large fighter hauled around describing a wide arc to the south as it manoeuvred into his stern hemisphere. He watch it turn and, as it began to threaten from his four o'clock, he pulled the control column roughly from left to right waggling his wings in an exaggerated gesture to show that he had seen the attack develop and that he acknowledged the threat. On a normal day he would have responded well before, throwing in a defensive turn, simulating popping chaff and flares and descending as low as he could. His mission today precluded any reaction but he wanted to ensure that the crew did not take home any gunsight film to confer bragging rights. It was all too common to receive a shot of a pipper embedded on the cockpit of a gently manoeuvring Jaguar. With little to maintain his interest the Phantom pilot hauled off and turned back south to continue his journey. He was well away from his normal haunts in the north and Nick wondered idly where he was heading.

Up ahead the a bank of cloud was building as the lone Jaguar flew towards the tail of the weather front. The cloud was set in a shallow layer with a distinct overcast forming a letter box between the rising ground of the Harz Mountains and the solid cloud deck. A distinct line marked the cloud tops above the bank and Nick estimated that the cloud formation was as yet only a few thousand feet thick. The question would be how far the front had progressed. If the met man was to be believed, it was through Gütersloh and already well into the Buffer Zone where he planned to turn north, hopefully remaining to the west of the clag. A glance at his map suggested that the met man's estimate of its progress might be optimistic. He relaxed for the time but knew that life in the cockpit was going to get much busier if the weather closed in. A quick check of his position over the ground confirmed that, at least his NAVWASS was on top form. The aircraft symbol matched his location exactly.

The rolling plains formed deeper gulleys as the ground rose into the mountains. There was still a distinct gap above the hill tops leaving an escape route if he was forced to pull up but the gap was slowly narrowing. The characteristics of a cold front meant that there would be little transition between the good conditions he was presently enjoying and the shit and corruption which generally follows the line of a cold front. He was now at the mercy of the met forecast and heading into the weather.

The deterioration, when it came, was rapid and unexpected. The met forecast had been over optimistic and the weather front had slowed as it hit the rising ground of the Harz Mountains. The letter box closed above him and, as he passed over the pretty rolling hills, the terrain began to rise rapidly ahead of him. A valley formed and the wide sides slowly narrowed, constricting his route ahead. On either flank the solid overcast touched the tops of the hillsides cutting off his escape routes to each side. He was being funnelled into the valley with its rapidly reducing girth and rising slopes. The reduction in visibility was almost instant and, within seconds, the cloying mists clinging to the tail end of the front enveloped the Jaguar and the bright blue rays of the sun disappeared, replaced by low lying clouds and poor visibility. Nick looked left and right searching for visual reference cues in order to keep the jet straight and level but the ground was rapidly disappearing in the mist. Only flickers of the ground were visible and he quickly developed an overpowering sense of disorientation as his references were denied. He nearly panicked. Fortunately, his flying drills were ingrained, developed over his years of training and he quickly transferred his attention, concentrating inside the cockpit, focussing on the flight instruments before him.

Wings level.

Stroke up the throttles into full reheat.

Pause.

Pull back smoothly to 60 degrees of climb . . . . .and hope.

He was flying blind relying completely on his instruments and the ground was only feet below him. He tensed, waiting for what seemed like the inevitable impact with the surface but the altimeter began to wind upwards, rapidly, as the power of the reheated Adour engines took sway. Within seconds he popped out above the weather passing through the solid tops into the bright blue clear air above and the crisis was over, instantly. His sigh of relief was audible and he realised that he was talking to himself, chiding, cajoling. Levelling at 5,000 feet now well above the solid deck, he followed the route on his NAVWASS sticking precisely to his pre-planned waypoints, albeit they were invisible below him, masked by the cloud deck.

He cursed audibly in his mask, the drama of a few minutes ago already forgotten. His rehearsal was blown and he resigned himself to a re-fly. Plan B he decided as he turned north hastily feeding a new waypoint into the kit. The bug on his compass swung around and he took up the new heading towards the eastern end of Low Flying Area 1. There were nine minutes to run to the new turn and, hopefully, he would find a gap in the clouds en route to allow him to let back down to low level.

Some minutes later, the NAVWASS showed him in a clear area to the west of the town of Minden skirting clear of the Hannover control zone. Threading around the puffy clouds he spotted an elusive gap and pushing the stick forward he eased back on the throttles to maintain 420 knots descending slowly towards the ground. His head moved rhythmically from side to side peering around the ironwork in the windscreen. He doubted any light aircraft would be venturing forth as yet with the weather conditions still marginal in this area but enough had gone wrong today to make him doubly cautious.

The ground had flattened out and the weather had improved. He was over flat terrain cut by a network of drainage ditches. At least he could run through his attack profile so that the trip was not entirely wasted. He would use the impromptu waypoint as the target. A few mental calculations and he had the coordinates for an ad hoc initial point which he fed into the kit. It would hardly be a set piece rehearsal but at least he might resurrect some value from the weather abort. During a loft attack he would not see the point on the ground which marked his target so the fact that he had chosen a railway station was of little relevance. The travellers waiting for their connection to Hannover Haupt Bahnhof would be blissfully unaware that they had been singled out for simulated Armageddon.

The Jaguar powered over the small mast which he had chosen as the IP, reflections from the Dümmersee glinting in the windscreen confirming his position. The electronic symbology in his head up display gyrated briefly, settling down as he selected toss mode. The time-to-go display showed three minutes to the pull up which, in turn, was four miles short of the target. Once the cue illuminated he would pull up to 60 degrees of climb and the weapon would automatically leave the pylon 15 seconds later following an arcing trajectory ahead of the jet. At the apex, a hard wingover would bring the Jaguar around onto the reciprocal heading descending hard for the deck to avoid the blast wave. The time of flight of the bomb was short so precision was vital if the airframe was not to suffer immeasurable stresses from a nuclear explosion. Ahead, the flat terrain was unremarkable and the fact that he was practising for oblivion did not register against the normality of life below. The seconds counted down and, as the readout reduced to zero, the display flashed prompting the pull. With the wings level he fed in full afterburner on both engines and the nose rose sharply into the sky. Checking forward, the climb bars registered the precise angle he had demanded and the altimeter wound upwards rapidly. He cross checked the switches for a final time confirming the armament safety lock was live. All was set.

At the last moment he realised that he was carrying a “shape”! What was he thinking? In his haste to re-plan the delivery he had forgotten the most fundamental aspect of safety. In his desire to train for real he had almost consented to toss a 1,000 lb practice thermonuclear bomb into a railway siding. He snapped the safety lock to safe just in time to prevent the practice weapon from leaving the pylon. The display occulted as it should and he realised, thankfully, that the light on the weapons control panel glowed reassuringly registering the continued presence of his deadly cargo. The "shape" was still onboard.

His mind was in turmoil. On the one hand he was relieved that he had avoided disaster by the skin of his teeth, not just once but twice. On the other hand his moral conflict returned. His mind flashed back to the planning room at Brüggen and he could see the layout of the airfield at

Zerbst in his mind's eye. Had his weapon been released for real he would have consigned thousands of people to a lingering death. Did the destruction really protect his airbase back on the Dutch border? He had rehearsed the argument so many times in his mind yet he would never rationalise cause and effect. Nuclear weapons were a necessary evil and in the face of a Soviet onslaught, there would be few other options to stem the tide of an advance. Despite that, the consequences of his actions were increasingly alien to him. The naivety of his training being taught to fly a jet aircraft had been overtaken by a harsh reality.

His thoughts returned to the cockpit with a start. The moralising could wait.

CHAPTER 15

Delta Dispersal, RAF Wildenrath.

The Duty Authoriser on the operations desk on Delta Dispersal stared at the classified signal that had just dropped onto the desk. The admin. clerk, unaffected by the news it foretold was already leaving, unconcerned at someone else's problem. The capitalised script was unequivocal. A Special Instruction had been issued by the Phantom Air Engineering Authority grounding the fleet with immediate effect. The speedbrake mounting brackets on one of the RAF's Phantoms had developed cracks in the supporting structure and were at risk of failing in flight. Every jet was to be inspected and a non-destructive test carried out before the next flight. It was hours of work for the engineers on each airframe.

He stroked his dampening brow analysing the implications when the final paragraph suddenly caught his eye. There was a risk of a rapid rolling moment in the event of a failure. If one speedbrake failed at high speed there was a small risk of departure from controlled flight. Nicely done. Catch 22 putting all the risk on him. Any sorties currently airborne were to be recalled and the crews instructed to return to base without further use of the speedbrakes. Nightmare!

He checked the board. Just Mike Limas 66 and 72 airborne at present. They were operating autonomously in Low Flying Area 2. His own squadron radio certainly wouldn't reach them up there even if they were monitoring the frequency which they would not be doing but he may be able to get a message through to them via the Control and Reporting Centre at Uedem. "Crabtree" was the control agency. He picked up the phone.

“Is that the Master Controller? . . . . . Sir, Flight Lieutenant Willis on the ops desk on 92 Squadron at Wildenrath. I need you to issue a recall for all my jets currently working in Area 2. It’s a flight safety recall so absolutely vital to get through to them.”

CHAPTER 16

Fifteen Minutes to Impact.

"Mike Lima 72 become Red 2."

"Red 2."

"All stations, Red formation, two F4s established on RCAP 2 at 1,500 feet."

The pair of Phantoms pulled up from low level and began a radar search of the airspace ahead. Minutes later Mac pulled hard towards his wingman timing his turn precisely. Razor in the other jet would be watching him intently and taking separation. The Phantom disappeared below his nose and a check confirmed that he was passing the 90 degree point in the turn. Perfect. As he craned his head over his shoulder clearing his flight path, he felt a slight thump as he nibbled the edge of the wake vortex from the other jet. He sensed rather than saw movement in his peripheral vision as the master caution captions on the cockpit coaming flashed angrily. He was working to capacity. It would have to wait.

"O2 Low caption," he heard from the back seat. "Selecting 100%."

Cockers pushed the toggle switch down on his chest-mounted oxygen regulator isolating himself from the outside cabin air and transferring exclusively to the oxygen supply in the bowels of the Phantom. He was still breathing. The gauge in the cockpit had dropped to zero. In the front, Mac steadied up on the reciprocal heading, his wingman back in perfect battle formation a mile away, line abreast. He hit the flashing caption to acknowledge the warning.

"I'm still breathing normally so it must be a gauge error," he heard from the pit. "Check your contents."

Mac glanced down. The gauge read zero.

"Checking."

He went through the same drill and, like his back seater, the life-giving air continued to flow. It could only mean one thing. He relaxed.

"Agreed. Looks like a gauge problem. The weather's wide open blue so I can't see us having to pull up. Are you happy to press on? We're still breathing."

"Affirmative, we can snag it on the ground. Can't miss this sortie can we?"

The mistake by the harassed liney back on the dispersal at Wildenrath had almost caused an aborted sortie.

*

A semblance of normality was returning to the cockpit of the Jaguar as Nick turned westerly skirting the northern edge of the Osnabruck Ridge. After the tribulations of the emergency pull up and the close call with the practice weapon he was grateful for a few minutes of relative calm. His jet was nicely trimmed out and sitting comfortably at 250 feet, his instruments pegged on parameters. He tweaked the throttles more from the need to stay active than from necessity. To the right, the North German Plain stretched out into the distance, flat and uninspiring. A factory chimney belched out black smoke which rose in a column until it petered out at about 2,000 feet. To his left the ground rose sharply to the crest along the escarpment providing a natural barrier between the two low flying areas. He would be concealed from anyone operating at low level to the south.

As he checked right to follow the natural line of the contours ahead he dropped the wing registering the cars on the autobahn below speeding along at over 100 miles per hour. It reinforced his intention to get out and about on his travels and see more of this pretty countryside from the ground rather than from his detached vantage point above.

He rapidly overhauled a light aircraft which tracked along the ridgeline, its pilot using the dominant feature as a navigation aid. It was a momentary distraction that had no bearing on his own progress. The pilot, unless he was particularly sharp, would be unaware of the military traffic below, the Jaguar rendered almost invisible by its tactical camouflage.

He needed to resurrect some value from this shambles and there was only one potential solution. He flicked through his frequency card on his kneeboard looking for the initial contact frequency for Nordhorn range.

CHAPTER 17

Ten Minutes to Impact.

The Phantoms pulled up from low level to establish the combat air patrol. The datum passed below the lead aircraft as it commenced its outbound leg, the radars in the noses of each aircraft scanning the airspace ahead. It was some minutes before the Buccaneers were due to check in on frequency but the area was likely to be busy given the weather conditions. With poor weather to the east all the traffic would be funnelled into the clearer conditions in the westerly low flying areas. The radars scanned the airspace out to the radar horizon a mere 27 miles but in the crisp visibility behind the weather front the crews could almost see that far ahead; an unusual phenomenon over the North German Plain.

Mac McKenzie in the lead Phantom looked over at his wingman who had stepped down to give a modicum of tactical separation. Squeezed by the light aircraft band above them, they could not climb any higher but, as the Buccaneers would be leaving Nordhorn range via the southerly gate, their holding pattern would be high enough to detect their arrival.

With the scope still devoid of contacts Mac signalled an early turn by waggling his wings prompting a hard turn towards by his wingman. Matching the manoeuvre Mac hauled the stick over and the G forces assailed his body forcing him down into the seat. The Phantom protested slightly as it hit 21 units angle of attack and he backed off. Better to save the effort for the engagement. His wingman passed close aboard disappearing below the nose, as Mac dropped the wing to clear below the Phantom. A turn was the most vulnerable manoeuvre and he had no desire to allow a roving fighter to creep up on them unannounced. He knew that Razor in the other jet would be matching his caution. Reefing back into the turn the numbers on his compass dragged around until the reciprocal heading registered. A short dash back to the datum and they should be perfectly positioned to meet the Buccaneers as they came off range.

"Anvil check."

"Two, three."

"Red this is Anvil."

"Anvil, Red, loud and clear on CAP."

"Red roger, Anvil departing the range, on track, on time."

"Red copied."

"I thought we were up against a pair of Buccs Cockers?"

"That's what they said in the briefing Boss. Did I hear three jets check in?"

"You did. Looks like a bit of shady play going on here. Either someone is acting like a third jet on the radio or we have extra company. Make sure you take a good look at the radar during the run in. If we have an extra player in the mix I want to know."

"Roger will do."

Cockers made a snap assessment. It was not unknown for the navigator in one of the Buccaneers to make it seem that there were more jets in the formation than there actually were. All was fair in love and war! The wait was short.

"Bogeys!"

Flash's monosyllabic call heralded the arrival of their playmates.

"045."

The pair of Phantoms eased around onto a closing heading.

"Low level. Multiples. Fast." He intoned quickly building the tactical picture.

By making the radio call, Flash had assumed control of the tactical engagement. Unless overridden by Cockers in the lead jet he would set up the intercept geometry. The pair immediately descended back towards the deck levelling at 250 feet and easing up to fighting speed. Heads in the front cockpits were now on gimbals hunting left and right around the ironwork which restricted the forward view from the Phantom cockpit. Minor adjustments were made unbidden. For real, there would be little value in making unnecessary radio calls which might attract the unwanted attention of a Soviet electronic warfare battalion. Erroneous calls would act like a beacon on the frequency and automatically cue a responsive jammer, obliterating the tactical frequency with electronic noise. The clipped transmissions, hopefully, would minimise the risk.

"Showing a pair."

The ante was raised.

"Target heading 240."

This was consistent with the Buccaneers planned flight path down through the low flying area back towards their base at Laarbruch. The lead Phantom eased out even further to the east widening the frontage of the formation.

"Bracket."

One simple word but conveying vital information about the plan. Flash would displace to the east expecting Mac and Cockers to fly outside the incoming formation and achieve a tactical bracket. Without an identification they would have to close inside visual acquisition range and identify their simulated targets as Buccaneers. Only at that point could they engage with a head-on Sparrow missile. If the identification came too late and they were too close, they would be committed to turn in behind and employ an infra-red guided Sidewinder missile for the kill. With the smoky Rolls Royce Speys and the massive planform of the Phantom, it was unlikely that they would be able to close unseen. A response from the defenders would mean having to work hard for the simulated kill as the defending crews employed manoeuvres and defensive electronic countermeasures to foil the shot.

Although the attack was developing well, why did Mac feel that all was not as it seemed? He glanced occasionally at the radar when his stretched capacity allowed. Operating so close to the ground and striving to maintain 250 feet, the glances were infrequent and the fuzzy display seemed unintelligible. The stream of tactical information came as a revelation as the back seater in the other jet continued with the commentary. His own back seater was disturbingly quiet.

"What do you see Cockers?" he pressed.

"I'm breaking out two. Our guy is 10 degrees right and the far guy 40 degrees right. Razor and Flash are on him."

"Speed?"

"Showing 450 knots."

It was like pulling teeth and he wished he was still flying with his old back seater who would have been talking at break neck speed by now. He would have to hope for an early visual.

"Confirm you still show only two contacts?"

"Affirmative. Only two."

A look across the formation and he sensed rather than saw the other Phantom begin its turn. Sure enough, the wing flashed and it began to ease in towards the extended flight path. Mac sensed the radar contacts were getting close. Sure enough the commentary from the other jet increased in both intensity and volume. Suddenly, he spotted the familiar profile of a Buccaneer in his one o'clock. The round intakes and high tail were unmistakable as was the height at which the jet was flying. He re checked his altimeter and sure enough, it read a solid 250 feet which cross checked with his radio altimeter. The incoming jet was way below and he had to drop the right wing to keep it in sight.

"Hostile, Hostile, Hostile," he called over the tactical frequency, his hand whipping back to the missile selector as the Sparrow selected and ready lights responded. The familiar engagement symbology appeared on his radar scope but it rapidly collapsed signifying that he had already passed inside the minimum engagement zone.

"Bogeys now!"

Razor pulled up and over his own quarry and Mac saw the side profile of the second Buccaneer as it flashed below his wingman. The pair turned hard towards each other, their intent to cross to the opposing side of the formation and engage the opposite defender hoping that the Buccaneers would run out in an attempt to disengage from the fight.

"Pulling high!" called Razor as the other Phantom flashed over the top, perilously close and dragging a wicked wake vortex behind. Mac's airframe shook as it hit the slipstream and he felt the effect hard through the controls. As he pulled back down earthwards he called his navigator to look out to guard against an unseen attacker. The call was based on gut feeling rather than intuition but proved astute. As he settled in behind the fleeing Buccaneer, his gunsight level on the horizon, he knew that he was at his most vulnerable. Never stay straight and level in the combat zone for more than 15 seconds was the old adage which had held true since the days of The Red Baron. To achieve a missile kill at low level would take at least that much time, if not longer.

He matched the flight path of the Buccaneer and positioned the aiming dot on the centreline. In the back, Cockers rejoiced noisily as he finally achieved a lock to the elusive low level radar blip. On the repeater scope in the front cockpit the Sidewinder steering dot that suggested control demands to the pilot, lurched downwards. With the dot centred in the circle indicating its seeker coverage, the missile would be offered the best chance to achieve an intercept course to its target. Crucially, in order for the seeker head to acquire its target in the first place, the dot would have to be dragged into the circle. The Buccaneer was at 100 feet - if it was at an inch - and to bring the dot into the centre would demand a hefty push towards the ground below. Mac prepared himself for the tricky manoeuvre.

"Break port!"

The command was short, sharp and very loud.

Mac reacted without hesitation all thoughts of taking the shot gone. He hit the burners, paused for a second to allow them to bite and reefed into a hard turn.

"Hunter six o'clock, range one mile."

It was already inside missile parameters.

"Flares, flares," called Cockers as he dispensed the infra-red countermeasures into the airflow behind. The tiny pyrotechnic decoys were designed to confuse a missile seeker head by presenting a more attractive target to the missile. The short sequence of decoys would ignite instantly on leaving the dispensers mounted on the rear of the missile pylons and fall behind and away from the Phantom, hopefully seducing the missile away from its path. If successful, the missile would strike the ground some way behind the jet. If not, its warhead would rip a stripe across the thin metal skin damaging internal systems and destroying the integrity of the airframe. Today, however, the flares were simulated and the missile shot taken only for practice.

"That'll be our mysterious third player," grunted Mac as he strained under the G forces, his head canted backwards over his shoulder in a vain attempt to see the attacking Hunter.

"Keep talking."

"Seven o'clock range one mile top up."

"Top up" meant Cockers could see the top surfaces of the attackers wing. Unless the attacking pilot had already launched a missile it meant the defensive turn had achieved its aim and he was unable to pull the nose on to fire a missile.

Mac held the turn, slowly making angles on his pursuer but knowing that the Hunter in this environment was more than a match for the turn performance of his own jet. Although the afterburners should give enough thrust to hold this turn, he would not make any further gains and just one small mistake would allow the Hunter pilot in for the kill. He needed help.

"Red 1 engaged. Single Hunter, bullseye 145 range 10."

"Red 2 hauling off, I have you visual."

The cavalry in the form of Razor and Flash, had dispatched their own Buccaneer and were on the way.

"Baron check."

"Two, three, four."

"Mike Lima Red formation this is Baron."

The accent was distinctly German.

"Baron go," grunted Mac as he held the Hunter just at the edge of the missile envelope. He pulled back on the stick angling the nose up and away from the ground but without taking it up into the vertical he could not take advantage of the superior thrust-to-weight ratio of the Phantom. The Hunter stuck tight.

"Baron is off range and repositioning for the first run. Will be at the start point in five minutes."

"Baron, Red, roger. Presently engaged but will be complete in three minutes and back to CAP."

"Baron roger. Baron running-in in five minutes."

Mac's casual response belied the intensity of his struggle. In his peripheral vision he spotted the familiar profile of his wingman's Phantom as it pulled up in an exaggerated wingover on the opposite side of the circle of joy. Although Mac was stuck in a predictable orbit, he was towing the Hunter in his wake in an equally predictable circle. Razor would be able to reposition and slot into a firing position which, unless the Hunter acknowledged the threat and countered, would lead quickly to a kill.

"Twenty seconds to kill," heard Mac over the tactical frequency."

"Gutsy move Biggles," he muttered.

True to his word, Razor flew a perfect lag pursuit roll high across the circle slotting into the saddle. The Hunter pilot intent on his kill failed to spot the new threat and remained in tow.

"Fox 2 on the Hunter passing west, Bullseye 045 range eight miles."

The short fight was over and the unexpected threat had been neutralised. The Buccaneers had barely been seen and had egressed, albeit, at the expense of a Sidewinder shot taken against one of them. As the pair of Phantoms pulled up and slotted back into battle formation the twin seat Hunter pulled up alongside Mac slotting into close formation. The pilot's oxygen mask dropped from his face and a huge grin spread across his face. Mac recognised an old friend from his days on the Tactical Weapons Unit at Chivenor. With a thumbs up the Hunter dropped back and descended back to low level accelerating to catch the pair of Buccaneers by now well ahead and into their recovery to Laarbruch.

The Hunters operated by the Buccaneer squadrons were two seat trainer aircraft pressed into service as there were no two stick trainer variants of the Buccaneer itself. Normally used for pilot check rides and instrument rating tests, the lack of an operational mission meant that the rare opportunities for the Buccaneer pilots to play in the highly manoeuvrable sports car were seen as a bonus. The fact that shots had been taken was of little consequence to the grinning bomber pilot. It had been fun.

*

Up ahead the towers of the enormous power station known to every aviator in West Germany as "Smokey Joe's" pumped smoke into the atmosphere. Knowing precisely where he was and with a simple straight track to the next waypoint, Nick's workload reduced considerably. He would avoid any fighters pre-target and see how he felt when he came off range. He might allow himself a few defensive manoeuvres if he came across any Phantoms as he ran back down through Area 2. The NAVWASS seemed accurate and for the first time today he felt really relaxed in the cockpit. With a new route entered into the kit he would run towards Smokey's, turn north and run up the eastern side of Nordhorn range up to the range entry point. He would fly a simple first run attack profile for a laydown. On second thoughts, with the "shape" loaded he had no intention of trying to be clever. The sortie had nearly been a "rolling goat" already. The weapon aiming computer was programmed for a WE 177C profile and he had no intention of making a second attempt to drop the practice weapon in error. He was sure that the range controller at Nordhorn would be absolutely delighted to find the inert simulated nuclear weapon on his target array! Perhaps a simple visually aimed practice bomb would be a smarter bet and he would just run through the motions. Maybe instead he'd throw in a strafe pass. At least he couldn't screw that up, or could he with the way his day had shaped up so far? No, it was an entirely different set of switchery positions to fire the gun and less chance for the "Law Unto Sod" to make a play.

Decisions taken he relaxed and even managed to take in the scenery for a brief moment.

CHAPTER 18

Five Minutes to Impact.

With the Buccaneers clear of the area the two Phantoms homed in on the distinctive mast at Osterwick re-establishing their combat air patrol with the lull in proceedings allowing a chance to catch up with some housekeeping. Both crews ran through routine checks confirming the systems aboard each jet were still functioning normally, there was enough fuel for the remaining engagement with the F-104s and recycling weapons systems to reselect the dummy air-to-air missiles they were carrying. As they approached the datum, a cross turn reversed the heading and they were once more heading north easterly in the direction of the impending threat.

"Bogeys!"

This time it was Cockers turn to control the shots and the transmission prompted the usual shot of adrenaline.

"050."

"Good boy," said Flash as he listened to the commentary from the lead Phantom. "Grab it by the balls and let's see what you can do."

The Phantoms descended back towards the sanctuary of low level, pushing up to fighting speed.

"Red for hook attack. Two crossover port," the young navigator called over the tactical frequency.

"Outstanding!" said Flash recognising the tactics the young navigator was using. "Just what I would have done."

"Targets heading 240. Multiple contacts. Final turn to starboard."

It was a classic tactic he had selected and the range between the two formations wound down.

In the lead Phantom Cockers was chatting away to his pilot calling the radar contacts and translating the information into positional cues to focus his pilot's eyes on the point in space where the threat should appear.

Out in battle formation Razor took full advantage of the unusually fine visibility. Used to flogging around in the murk of a West German winter day, the crystal clear skies allowed him to widen the formation and still keep visual contact on his leader. In his back seat, Flash monitored the progress of the intercept ready to take over in an instant if the young tyro in the lead jet screwed up. Both Phantoms pulled up slightly to ensure that the radar could still see over the ridgeline which barred progress. Fly too low and they would lose the targets behind the ridge. Too high and they would be highlighted against the bright blue sky.

Cockers positioned the acquisition markers over the nearest target and selected half action using the trigger on the hand controller in the back cockpit. The radar froze in azimuth directing the power of the AN/AWG 12 radar along the designated bearing focussing on the target. After a swift electronic calculation inside the radar's electronic brain, the full locked-up symbology appeared and the target marker settled down. Happy with the information Cockers broke lock and the radar returned to its lazy scan left and right.

"Ten miles," he called over the radio.

They moved into the terminal phase of the intercept.

*

Nick hugged the contours of the ridgeline hidden from view of the prying electronic eyes of the Phantoms to the south. A walker standing atop the escarpment watched his progress through a telephoto lens snapping away. The pictures would resurface some days later as exhibits.

The familiar rattle of his ARI 18223 radar warning receiver disturbed the quiet of the cockpit and a series of rhythmic pulses rose in volume. Glancing at the cathode ray tube threat display on the coaming, a vector strobed away in his one o'clock announcing the presence of the Hawk surface-to-air missile system which had been set up to catch unwary aviators. Positioned a few miles from the natural barrier it formed a choke point to trap aircraft flying in the lee of the escarpment. Its persistent attention intensified and the random pulses settled into a set rhythm.

When it came, the lock-on was unmistakable. The pulses formed a steady, intense beat and the accompanying screech of the audio warning with the CW light illuminated on the threat display, signified the presence of the continuous wave tracking beam which would guide the bulky surface-to-air missile to its target. Nick's natural reaction would have been to break away from the threat vector placing the target tracking radar on the beam but his escape route to the south was barred by the ridge. Pulling up would take him away from the protection of ground clutter which would make the task of the missile tracking system infinitely easier. Framed against the skyline he would be an easy target.

Choosing the lesser of two evils, he turned to place the threat directly on the nose. It had been a carefully constructed trap expertly implemented by the missile crew using the terrain to make their target predictable. Although he was sweetening the shot against him, he would close the range on the Hawk as quickly as possible, hopefully entering the minimum range ring before the automatic firing program could complete its sequence. He hoped his jamming pod under the wing was doing its business. The threat display taunted him as he held the heading firm, the vector flashing menacingly, the audio warning blaring its challenge. Suddenly, all was silent and the Hawk tracking radar broke lock. Dropping the wing he looked below and was rewarded with sight of the fire unit, standing out clearly against the green fields below. The camouflage netting which had been pulled over the support vehicles had been drawn back to reveal the twin discs of the squat target tracking radar which now slewed around attempting to predict his egress heading. He held the angle of bank and pulled back on the stick reefing the fighter bomber around in a defensive break. Turning through 90 degrees he aimed directly for the safety of the ridgeline. Knowing that the continuous wave tracker was immune to ground clutter he anticipated the return of the apocalyptic warning as the hidden operator on the ground reacquired. Nothing came. The threat warner remained utterly silent. As he approached the brow of the hill he overbanked pulling back towards the ground to remain shielded and resumed station in the lee, once more hugging the contours.

His carefully constructed plan for the sortie was in tatters. A fallback was needed to resurrect some vestige of value from the shambles. He switched frequency on the radio box and listened briefly making sure the channel was quiet before hitting the transmit button.

"Nordhorn, Four Alpha Tango Echo, good afternoon."

"Four Alpha Tango Echo," Nordhorn, good afternoon, loud and clear, go ahead."

The English accent was welcoming.

"Four Alpha Tango Echo is a single Jaguar presently 20 miles east of Hopsten, heading 270. Can you accept me for a first run attack at minute 15?"

"Four Alpha Tango Echo affirmative. Our last serial has cancelled and we have a free slot. Call me approaching the IP for further instructions."

"Four Alpha Tango Echo, willco thanks."

Well, if he had to re-fly the profile he may as well get as much out of the rest of the mission as possible. There must be some fighters in Area 2 who would like to play.

CHAPTER 19

Three Minutes to Impact.

"All stations, all stations this is Crabtree on Guard. Transmitting blind. Recall message for all Mike Lima callsigns. From your operators, you are to return to base immediately. If you receive this message come up TAD 451 and acknowledge."

"Did you get that Cockers," Mac asked, the message garbled and indistinct in his headset.

"Negative, unreadable."

"Red 2 did you get that last transmission?" he queried over the radio.

"Negative, transmission broken and unreadable," Razor responded.

The Phantom radio was notoriously poor at high frequencies and, particularly, at low level. Missing transmissions was a fact of life in the noisy cockpit.

"It can't have been important. They'll retransmit if it was," said Mac.

It was to be a fatal error to ignore the recall.

*

The Osnabruck Ridge was fast approaching and beyond lay the F-104 formation. As the intensity of the commentary from the lead navigator increased the pilots pushed the throttles into minimum reheat to kill the smoke plume and to reduce their visual signature. In fact the gesture was largely wasted as they were barely visible to the inbound bombers.

Although lacking radar warning equipment, the pilots in the F-104s were sufficiently savvy to know that they were easily visible to the pulse Doppler radars in the Phantoms and that, for real, Sparrow missiles would be launched beyond visual range and the first that they would know of an attack would be one of their number exploding in flames. Although the timing would be guess work, at the mission briefing they had briefed a procedural turn through 90 degrees at the later stages of the engagement in order to confuse the velocity tracking of the Phantom radars. As they approached the Osnabruck Ridge, Uli Müller in the lead aircraft called an in-place turn and the four Starfighters made wide turns to the west. Holding the manoeuvre for twenty seconds he took the opportunity to scan the horizon above the ridge for the tell tale smoke plume of an attacking Phantom. The horizon was clear. He called the in-place turn back onto track and the formation resumed its inbound heading. Four pairs of eyes in the sleek bombers were scanning the skyline for the elusive first contact which would confer bragging rights at the ensuing debrief.

The horizon remained clear. Still some miles distant, and outside their field of view, they had no chance of detecting the Jaguar hugging the ridgeline and concealed by the terrain beyond.

The three formations converged.

CHAPTER 20

One Minute to Impact.

"Lost contact."

It was a navigator's worst nightmare. Into the last phases of an engagement and the target disappears. Flash glanced through the quarter light and his view was obscured by the ridgeline. At least that explained it. They were too low and the ridge was obscuring the targets from view.

"Pulling up for contact," Cockers called over the tactical frequency. "Last seen twenty right, estimate range eight miles."

"Negative!"

The intervention was harsh and came from his own front cockpit.

"Red, stay low and I'll call pulling up."

Concise.

"Crest the ridge and pull through," Mac called to his wingman. His intent was clear. Razor knew where the inbound targets should appear and he wanted to remain unsighted at the entry to the fight. He would rather accept a stealthy approach over the advantage of radar contact. He would need to time the pull up carefully. Too early and he risked pulling back down into the ridge and certain destruction. Too late and he would balloon at the apex and announce his entry into the fight allowing the prey to slip away behind the ridgeline. Get it right and they would be rolling out behind just as the F-104s were crossing the ridge heading south. The tables would be turned and it would be the German defenders who would be presenting their tails to the threat as they popped over the ridge.

He tensed as the escarpment grew in his peripheral vision. The rules demanded that he give the ridge a safety margin of 250 feet lateral separation. He would push that limit to the extreme if it gave him a tactical advantage.

CHAPTER 21

Thirty Seconds to Impact.

The flock of birds took flight without warning; a massive congress of common ravens rising in a whirling mass of black bodies. The sky ahead of Nick's Jaguar became opaque and it was impossible to find a way through the dense mass of swirling birds. He began a gentle pull up to clear the pandemonium but, immediately, he felt the impact of a bird on the fuselage. The central warning panel burst into life and flashed its ominous message as the right hand engine wound down. Within a few seconds, he smelled the distinctive aroma of cooking flesh from the raven ingested by the engine.

Nick increased the pull anxious to encourage his damaged fighter bomber away from the ground below and to give time to assimilate the problem. The RPM on the right was dropping rapidly and he felt the immediate retardation from the loss of thrust. With the pull up underway, the speed began to wash off alarmingly and he pushed the left engine into reheat to stabilise the deceleration. The speed pegged at 280 knots. As the windscreen lightened there was another massive crack and the left hand side of the windshield shattered as a bloodied carcass thrashed through the hole striking him on the visor. Luckily the dark visor absorbed the majority of the impact, but it broke the fasteners and the protective shield detached from the helmet. The clear visor beneath protected his face from the remnants of the bird but the impact had stunned him. An ear shattering wind rush assailed his senses. Momentarily startled, he shook his head to clear his vision and looked down at the array of warning lights, struggling to make sense of the mayhem. Pull up, wings level, altimeter increasing, speed at 280 he chanted to himself. It was bad but not terminal. At least he was still flying. A radio call. He needed to put out a Mayday call.

*

Mac watched Razor and Flash pull up into the vertical, framed against the steeply rising topography. He matched the manoeuvre a few seconds later, plugging in the afterburners, his wings parallel to the looming ridgeline ahead. Vaguely aware of trees which dropped quickly out of sight beneath his nose, the green was replaced by clear blue sky as he climbed. With the horizon impinging on his peripheral vision he glanced down at the attitude indicator checking the angle of climb at 60 degrees nose up and pulling the throttles back to min burner. He hit 420 knots prompting a snap roll that turned the jet inverted and pulled back hard for the horizon, looking up into the canopy above the windscreen arch as the ground replaced the sky. The fields beyond the ridge formed a pretty tableau but to carry on pulling would lead to oblivion. The fields and hedge lines skated across his line of sight as the nose canted crazily back earthwards. As he deselected afterburner with the speed rapidly increasing, he adjusted his rate of descent, looking ahead through the canopy to try to spot the F-104s which should be just the other side of the ridge. Alongside, just half a mile away, Razor synchronised his manoeuvre descending rapidly still inverted towards the weeds where he would be less conspicuous and, more importantly, less vulnerable to attack.

CHAPTER 22

Impact.

Still inverted, Mac was suddenly distracted by a flashing master caution caption. It was the most inopportune moment. The intensity of events in executing the manoeuvre prevented him from reaching up to cancel the warning but the amber caption alerted him to a speedbrake failure. It was a rare occurrence but, at that minute, absolutely critical. Although he had cancelled the burners the speed was building rapidly and he needed the speedbrakes to limit the acceleration. He watched as the airspeed indicator increased rapidly through 550 knots realising that unless checked, the Phantom was easily capable of exceeding Mach 1 in this regime. Dropping a sonic boom over the German countryside with the damage that would ensue did not bear thinking about. He pulled the control column hard left to return the Phantom upright but, as his mind tussled with the implications and still distracted by the speedbrake caption, a sixth sense kicked in.

*

As Nick struggled with his birdstrike drills his head moved rapidly around the cockpit, his hands flashing hurriedly moving switches and feeling the response from the sluggish airframe. Had he craned his head upwards he would have seen the Phantom descending rapidly from above his aircraft but, even if he had seen it, it was too late to prevent the inevitable. The heavy fighter slashed through his flight path and, with a grinding of metal, mayhem turned to crisis in mere milliseconds. The result was cataclysmic.

*

There was no warning, just a massive thump through the airframe and the vague image of a black shape passing rapidly through Mac's field of vision, climbing tentatively if erratically into the air above. The master caution erupted in a cacophony of noise and an array or red and amber captions which were indecipherable at that moment, lit the central warning panel: PC1, PC2, Pitch Aug Off, LH Gen Out Bus Tie Open. Impossible. . . . .

*

Unbeknown to the Jaguar pilot his right wing had sliced through the Phantom's stabilator causing both flight control surfaces to detach from their respective airframes. Deprived not only of lift from the right wing, the ailerons and flaps had been lost in the collision and normal control was impossible. Hydraulic fluid pumped from the severed utilities lines causing other services to die in sympathy.

*

The Phantom began to roll uncomfortably and Mac struggled with the controls forcing the stick hard over to check the rotation. The jet continued to roll in the opposite direction to his demands. Why was it rolling? What had happened? He would not be able to hold it for long. What he could not know was that the stabilator which provided pitch control, had disintegrated leaving just the spoilers and ailerons on the wings to rotate the jet around its longitudinal axis. The Phantom was barely controllable.

"Prepare to Eject," he called to Cockers in the back seat anticipating the inevitable. He forced the stick over to the limit of travel but still the jet failed to respond.

"Eject, Eject, Eject."

No fanfare, no discussion, no questions.

*

Deprived of most of the wing structure, the Jaguar began a lazy roll to the right. Nick checked the stick in the centre but there was no response from the controls. The nose had sliced down after the impact with what he thought might have been a Phantom and the jet was now in a gentle, rolling descent. Nothing he did made any difference as the sky replaced the ground in a regular repetitive rotation, the inexorable descent towards the fields below unstoppable. His visor was already a mess after the birdstrike and his flying suit was covered in blood but at least it would provide a modicum of protection. With no control over the stricken fighter bomber and the ground rapidly approaching, his decision was easy. He braced, locked back the "go forward" lever and pulled the handle. The wind rush as he rode up the rails was almost instant. He blacked out.

*

There was a loud crack and the Phantom's rear canopy separated cleanly whipping back into the airflow despite the rolling momentum. The rear seat followed seconds later as Cockers was propelled up the extending seat rail into the roiling airflow.

Mac struggled for a few more seconds and, slowly, the jet seemed to be responding but he was still inverted and 60 degrees nose down. The altimeter unwound rapidly and he was vaguely aware of 300 feet registering in his subconscious. Was he still inside the seat limits with this rate of descent he thought irrelevantly? He had left it very late to eject. His hand reached down for the seat pan handle while maintaining his superhuman pressure on the control column. At the last moment; revelation. He kicked in full rudder in the opposite direction and the jet responded instantly, rolling rapidly to the right and flicking momentarily upright. He braced, placed both hands on the ejection seat handle and pulled. There was a loud bang as his own canopy departed and he felt the brutal force, as first the gun and then the rocket pack fired, setting the seat on its upward trajectory. As he cleared the canopy rails he was conscious of the spinning horizon once more and the rapid roll that had again placed the earth above him. His seat was now powering with a force of 40G downwards towards the ground. Clear of the stricken jet, he was vaguely aware of the Phantom still plunging earthwards, inverted.

Cockers regained consciousness, his black out temporary, an inevitable function of the 40 G forces he had experienced as he was lifted from the stricken Phantom. He pulled hard on the parachute risers swinging around as he descended beneath the multi coloured parachute. He flicked up the dark visor which had lowered automatically under the g loads during the ejection. Below him the doomed jet headed earthwards its grey underbelly stark against the green backdrop of fields. He looked around for another parachute seeing nothing.

A bright flash and smoke registered in his peripheral vision as he swung uncomfortably beneath the parachute, the yellow survival pack hanging from the lanyard acting as a massive pendulum. He missed the moment at which the Phantom struck the ground but a dense plume of black smoke rose from the ground at the point of impact. At each rotation the pall increased in height. His stomach sank.

Razor and Flash watched the unfolding scene from above. From their elevated position two plumes of smoke rose from twin crash sites where each jet had gone down. The strident tones of multiple emergency locator beacons in their headphones crowded for attention on the International Distress Frequency.

*

The fuselage of the wounded jet, its cockpit empty, hammered through the trees causing an ugly rift in the neat tree line. The flat trajectory, the earlier gyration damped out, meant that the impact, when it occurred, was less violent. Inverted, the fin was ripped off on first contact and became the most recognisable feature in the debris trail. The nose struck next and peeled back leaving the blunt bulkhead to plough a furrow ahead of the slowing hulk. Parts of the wings had disintegrated under the massive forces exerted on the airframe peeling apart like ripe fruit scattering shards of fractured metal in its wake. The carnage was accompanied by the violent and unearthly shrieking of tortured metal that would have set teeth on edge had anyone been close enough to witness it. Birds, ironically more ravens, took flight from their nests in the tree tops, upset at the sudden disturbance to their previously ordered existence. The camouflaged hulk came rapidly to a halt clouds of smoke rising from its last resting place leaving only the flat underbelly of the war machine visible above the sides of the ploughed furrow. A store which may have been a gun pod or a bomb remained attached to the centreline pylon, its continued presence a miracle after the intensity of the crash. The markings on the green painted aerodynamic casing, remarkably undamaged, would cause consternation until its status was determined.

A calm descended once again over the tranquil German meadow as a car slowed at the barred gate that provided the only access to the field and a worried face emerged from the driver's window as he peered towards the crash site. A heated exchange with his passenger followed before it sped off, its occupants searching for the nearest public phone box anxious to unburden themselves of their troubling news. Some miles to the north a second plume of smoke rose into the crisp afternoon air, marking the harbinger of further destruction.

*

Overhead, a lone Phantom flew slowly by dipping its wing almost in tribute. With the crash site located, the intricate search and rescue mechanism leaped into action. Within minutes the first helicopter was converging on the scene.

*

Uli Müller in the lead F-104 adjusted the scale on his altimeter changing the regional pressure setting to the new value. He adjusted his height back to 500 feet cursing the politically correct faction in his country that demanded that he fly at this height, almost twice the height of the Brits he was working with today. Whilst they could fly at 250 feet in the low flying area, he was limited to 500 feet as a sop to the Socialists and the Greens. There was a world of difference between flying and fighting at the two heights. That step down to 250 seemed small but life was far more demanding at the lower height and mistakes less easily forgiven. More importantly, if he ever had to penetrate the Inner German Border on an operational mission, it would be the difference between life and death. Surviving at 500 feet was about as likely as a pheasant surviving a line of guns.

For what seemed like the tenth time he scanned his formation. His wingman was glued in position about a mile abeam. The trailing pair were tucked in and he could just see the jet in his eight o'clock if he craned his head around. At this height it stood out against the skyline beautifully. In the absence of a radar warning receiver his eyes were making up for this deficiency and he scanned the horizon ahead for the tell tale smoke trail of the approaching Phantoms. They were on CAP as the formation leader had confirmed when he had checked in a few moments ago. His tactics were imprinted in his brain and where he spotted the threat would dictate which direction he would turn.

What appeared in his peripheral vision was not at all what he had expected. Suddenly, a plume of dark smoke rose from below casting a silent pall over the landscape as it billowed in the gentle breeze. In the relatively calm conditions its passage skywards was sharply defined, pencil thin; a signal of doom.

Whatever had transpired it was not good news. His track would take him within a mile of what he now realised was a crash site. At that moment another plume rose from his peripheral vision. There were two jets down. He pulled back on the stick clearing the way ahead anticipating the presence of the Phantoms he had expected to meet. The lone Phantom appeared in his two o'clock clearly visible above the ridgeline carrying out a gentle orbit.

"Baron, Guard, Guard, Go!"

He selected the distress frequency on his radio box. A pause.

"Baron check."

"Two, three, four."

"All loud and clear, break. Mayday, Mayday, Mayday, Baron formation relaying. Presently 25 miles northeast of Hopsten heading 180 at 1,500 feet. Two jets down in my vicinity declaring an emergency and requesting SAR cover immediately."

"Baron formation Hopsten Approach on Guard acknowledged. Say again your position."

"Presently 25 miles northeast of you. The first incident bears 160 estimate range five miles. The second bears 240 range four miles. I see smoke in both locations. Request immediate assistance."

"Baron acknowledged, understand smoke in your vicinity. Scrambling search and rescue immediately. Orbit in your present position and standby this frequency."

His formation had closed in and now held loosely in echelon formation. The long undulating string of Starfighters was too unwieldy.

"Baron check your fuel."

The replies were very similar to his own fuel state.

"Baron three and four return to base independently. Baron two remain with me. Baron three, advise our operators of the situation and that we are holding here to provide assistance."

"Baron three roger to en route. Best of luck Uli."

Müller watched the other Phantom as it orbited the scene.

"Hopsten Approach, Mike Lima 72 on Guard, visual the 104s, holding at 1,500 feet and visual the two crash sites. Mike Lima 66 is down at my present location. I suspect he hit another aircraft, type unknown. Standing by for instructions."

The frequency was quiet as the controller digested the implications. His day had suddenly become markedly more complicated.

EPILOGUE

Hounslow, England.

The two figures strode purposefully towards the front door of the neat bungalow, poker faces set, body language neutral. It was a task neither relished but a tradition long held in the Service. The curtains twitched as they approached. The door slowly opened before they had even knocked. A blank face met their gaze.

"Mrs Gleason?"

The grey haired woman nodded mutely the look of concern in her eyes heightened by the sight of the dog collar.

"Is your son Nick Gleason, a member of the Royal Air Force?"

She nodded still silent.

"May we come in?"

*

OC A Flight walked into the Squadron Registry.

"Have you seen the file for the Form 540, Corporal?"

"Let me check Sir."

The corporal picked up his document register and flicked through the pages.

"No Sir, Flight Lieutenant Gleason signed it out this morning and didn't hand it back."

"Oh bloody hell. . . . ."

*

The gathering in the bar at Wildenrath was raucous. Flying had been suspended the moment the crash had been notified and the Squadron had been locked down. The Boss and the flight commanders had immediately gone into a huddle, the key documents had been impounded as required by the accident procedures and the entire dispersal had gone into limbo. It was that terrible period when facts were scarce and speculation rife. Slowly the news had filtered through. Mac and Cockers had ejected safely. Cockers was entirely unaffected and, reportedly, ready for another trip although Mac had come perilously close. His seat had separated just feet above the ground and he had swung only once in his 'chute before landing hard. He would certainly be a few inches shorter than he was at the start of the day but he was alive, if not a little shaken.

*

Mac and Cockers strode into the bar almost as if it was a normal evening and that the events of the last few hours had not happened. Razor and Flash were first to intercept them and pints of foaming Dortmunder were rapidly thrust into welcoming hands. The first beer never touched the sides. After medical checks, the crew had been released from Wegberg Hospital and shipped back to Wildenrath in a staff car. Although the Board of Inquiry had already convened they had not yet been called to discuss the accident but it would not be long before the President of the Board caught up with them. The medical team may have been a tad hasty to discharge them so quickly but there was always time for a beer. Discussions about the accident were, studiously, avoided knowing that to do so might prejudice the outcome. It was as if they had arrived fresh from a sortie debrief rather than from a hospital bed.

It was less than fifteen minutes before the Station Provost Marshal strode into the room, identified the two crew members he had been instructed to find and ushered Mac and Cockers quietly from the bar heading for a hastily convened conference room in Operations Wing. Razor and Flash merged into the crowd knowing that it would not be long before the Provost Marshal returned with instructions to terminate their short lived freedom. They would also be witnesses to the accident and be required to give evidence. It would be a long night for the crews involved.

It would be an equally long night for the rest of the aircrew in the bar. At Wildenrath, the loss of the Jaguar pilot would be keenly felt but the survival of their comrades was cause for celebration. At Brüggen the scene was being repeated in the Officers' Mess bar where the pilots toasted their lost comrade, each coping with the loss of their fellow flyer in the traditional way. Private grief would follow the bluster. It was what they would expect of their friends and colleagues if ever they "bought the farm".

*

"Let's get down to business. I'm Wing Commander Pat Stripling and I'm presently the Boss of 6 Squadron at Coltishall. For my sins I've been nominated as President of the Board of Inquiry."

The two other newly appointed Board members sat around the small table in the office in Joint Headquarters at RAF Rheindahlen. Outside, the street lights glowed brightly as they resigned themselves to a long evening ahead. Dinner would be an impossible luxury tonight. The female WRAF engineering officer had made the short trip down from RAF Gütersloh that afternoon whilst the two aircrew officers had been collected by an HS 125 commuter jet from their respective bases in UK and whisked across the Channel, landing at Wildenrath. The Junior Board member was a Phantom navigator from RAF Coningsby.

"I've just come out from a meeting with the Commander in Chief and his position is quite clear. If I was to paraphrase his words it would be that he doesn't plan to become a martyr to the cause. Let's just say that he was less impressed that a "shape" has been discovered hanging on a wreck in a field in Northern Germany. His instructions are that we dig into the supervisory aspects of this accident quite closely. Let's hope every "i" has been dotted and every "t" crossed or a few careers might be on the line."

“Any suggestion that it was other than a straight forward mid-air collision Sir?”

“No, first impression reports from those on the ground suggest an unfortunate coming together. Both crash sites have been sealed and each base is responsible for its own site. I’ve already spoken to the Master Controller at Crabtree and he’s impounded the tapes of the Phantom’s tactical frequency. The Jaguar was operating as a singleton so there’s no voice recording for him. The Phantom doesn’t have an accident data recorder so it will be down to us to piece together the facts as best we can. We’ll meet the Air Accident Investigator at the crash site tomorrow. The C in C has put a helicopter at our disposal so we’ll fly up there first thing. John, you need to get across to Wildenrath and Brüggen tonight and impound all the relevant documents both operations and engineering so that we can start to check them. Kate, you need to check with the staff here and pick up copies of all the relevant Air Staff Instructions to compare. I need to look at my instructions from the C in C and make sure I understand his directive. I'll start the preliminary interviews. We can’t go off half cocked. Any questions at this stage?"

Heads shook.

"OK I'd best get off to Wegberg and interview the Phantom crew.”

"You're not going to like this Sir but I just heard that the doctor released them an hour ago. Their injuries were not significant so he let them go home. The Provost Marshal has just found them in the bar at Wildenrath."

The President's look spoke volumes. It would indeed be a long night.

ABOUT THE AUTHOR

David Gledhill joined the Royal Air Force as a Navigator in 1973. After training, he flew the F4 Phantom on squadrons in the UK and West Germany. He was one of the first aircrew to fly the F2 and F3 Air Defence Variant of the Tornado on its acceptance into service and served for many years as an instructor on the Operational Conversion Units of both the Phantom and the Tornado. He commanded the Tornado Fighter Flight in the Falkland Islands and worked extensively with the armed forces of most NATO nations. He has published a number of factual books on aviation topics and a series of novels in the Phantom Air Combat series set during the Cold War.

AUTHOR'S NOTE

The layman's impression of life on a fast jet squadron might be of steely eyed killers trained to the peak of efficiency spending every waking moment in the cockpit. Life in reality was a lot different.

It is doubtful if pilots such as Nick Gleason would have harboured such morbid fears. To the layman a nuclear weapon is a fearful solution in war and represents a breakdown in the political will to resolve a crisis. To a target planner it is merely another tool in the armoury, albeit with far reaching implications when used. Designers over the years worked relentlessly to add destructive power to a single delivery and the advent of nuclear weapons was a step in that evolution. Even so, any first use of the nuclear armoury would have been a watershed for NATO. It was a genie which, once unleashed, could not be put back in its bottle. For the Soviets, nuclear weapons were an integral part of military doctrine and few doubted that a Third World War would see them employed across West Germany in order to neutralise the western military machine. Exercises followed a depressingly familiar script always culminating in a nuclear exchange and hours dressed in nuclear, biological and chemical warfare suits and gas masks. Nevertheless, it would be an automaton who did not question the ethics of destruction.

The central theme of Impact is distraction. Flying a fast jet demands utmost concentration and decisions in the cockpit often have to be taken instantly and must be right. The margin between success and failure is narrow and the implications of an error can be fatal, particularly when operating on the limits or close to the ground. Aircrew were often seen as precious and self-centred by non aviators but simple distractions before a mission might be taken into the cockpit diverting attention away from the primary aim. When these factors affected performance, supervisors had to take note and, sometimes, take action. Failure to recognise when frustration boiled over into distraction might lead to disaster. I feel certain that anyone who served on a squadron would recognise at least one incident in this novella and would have experienced it personally. I have studied a number of accidents during supervisory training where lack of intervention and a failure to break the chain of events led to the loss of a valuable aircraft and, sadly, on occasion, an even more valuable crew. It was, and is, drummed into military flying supervisors the world over.

I am not a nuclear weapons expert nor did I ever serve on a ground attack or nuclear strike squadron, my experience being purely in the air-to-air role. The details of the Jaguar nuclear weaponeering and tactics are, therefore, entirely fictional and possibly inaccurate. I hope they appear convincing and add to the drama of the narrative.

Happily Impact is fiction. I am not aware of any mid air collisions between a Phantom and a Jaguar although mid air collisions were all too common at the height of the Cold War as crews trained hard to hone the elusive combat edge. The events I described are entirely fictional and the players in the story are products of my over fertile imagination.

GLOSSARY

Ab-initio. A first tour pilot or navigator newly graduated from training.

Altex. Alternative exercise.

ARI. Airborne radio installation.

Ascot. A callsign used by RAF transport aircraft.

Bogey. A hostile aircraft.

"Bought the farm". An aircrew phrase meaning to die in a military accident. Literal meaning to buy the plot on which the aircraft crashed.

Buffer Zone. A strip of airspace acting as a buffer between the airspace of NATO and the Warsaw Pact. The Air Defence Interception Zone was the final buffer.

BX. Base exchange. The shopping mall at an American Air Force base.

Bullseye. A reference point from which targets are reported within and between formations and a controller.

CAP. Combat air patrol.

Charlie fit. A Phantom carrying two external fuel tanks under the wings.

C in C. Commander In Chief.

CW. Continuous wave. A tracking beam for semi-active air-to-air missiles.

Convex. The training phase on a squadron leading to being declared operational. Literally, conversion exercise.

Crabtree. A callsign for a German control and reporting centre.

Dzus fastener. A commercial quick release fastener which attached some panels to a Phantom.

FLM. Flight line mechanic known as a "liney" or "Flem".

Form 540. The squadron operations record.

FOURATAF. Fourth Allied tactical Air Force.

Fox , Fox 2 and Fox 3. Fox 1 a Sparrow or Skyflash head-on missile, Fox 2 a Sidewinder and Fox 3 a gun shot. These definitions are different on modern fighter squadrons.

Guard. The callsign for the International Distress Frequency. For military aircraft it was 243.0 MHz and for civilian aircraft 121.5 Mhz. The frequency was "studded" on a fighter radio so that it could be selected with one action.

HAS. Hardened aircraft shelter.

Hat on interview. A formal interview, its name coming from the fact the person receiving the "bollocking" would wear a hat denoting the severity.

HQ P&SS. Headquarters of the Provost and Security Branch of the RAF.

ID. Identification card.

IFF. Identification friend or foe. An electronic identification system.

INAS. Inertial navigation and attack system.

IP. Initial point. A navigation feature short of the target from which an attacking crew would begin precision navigation and timing to ensure an accurate arrival over the target.

ISS. Individual Studies School. Staff training for junior officers. The reading and writing course.

Lag pursuit roll. A basic fighter manoeuvre.

LAU. Launcher acquisition unit. A missile rail.

LH Gen Out Bus Tie Open. An electrical failure leaving the Phantom without some functions powered by the electrical system.

LOX. Liquid oxygen.

Man A. The leading flight line mechanic for a see-off. Man B was the No. 2.

MATZ. Military air traffic zone.

Mike Lima. The two word callsign for Wildenrath based aircraft. Other NATO bases had similar callsigns for example, Alpha Lima denoted a Belgian aircraft from Beauvechain.

MSD. Minimum safe distance. The bubble around a low flying aircraft. A pilot had to maintain a safe separation from all obstacles by at least the MSD.

MT. Motor transport.

NATO. North Atlantic Treaty Organisation.

NAVWASS. Navigation and weapon aiming sub-system.

NCO. Non-commissioned officer.

OC A Flight. The flight commander for A Flight. Normally there were two flights on a fast-jet squadron.

ORP. Operational readiness platform. A hardstanding close to the runway.

PC1, PC2. Primary flying control systems operated by hydraulic pressure.

PEC. Personal equipment connector.

PIREP. Pilots report.

Pitch Aug. The pitch stability augmentation system on the Phantom.

Playmate. Another cooperating aircraft involved in a mission.

Playtex. A separation manoeuvre involving breaking out from close formation into line abreast formation. It takes its name from the lingerie advertisement whose catch phrase was to "lift and separate".

QFE. A pressure setting applied to the altimeter to read height above the runway touchdown point.

QNH. A pressure setting applied to the altimeter to read height above mean sea level.

QRA. Quick reaction alert known as "Battle Flight" at RAF Wildenrath. Alert jets were held at high readiness states ready to scramble.

RAFAIR. An international callsign for an RAF aircraft.

RCAP. Radar combat air patrol.

Rolling Goat. Rolling Goat f^&*. A rude expression to describe a screw up, the final expletive omitted.

RPM Gauge. The engine gauge which monitored revolutions per minute on the engine.

RTB. Return to base.

Sangar. A ground defence post.

SAR. Search and rescue.

Shape. A codeword for a practice nuclear weapon. Similar in shape and size to the real weapon.

Soft accommodation. Squadron buildings constructed from light building materials. "Hard" accommodation was built from reinforced concrete.

SOP. Standard operating procedure.

SOXMIS. The Soviet Military Liaison Mission.

Stick. A nickname for the pilot. Navigators were sometimes nicknamed "Scope".

Stud. A preset on the radio box allowing a frequency to be set with a single button selection, for example Stud 1 is the Tower frequency.

"Squipper". A nickname for a safety equipment fitter.

Tac Check. Tactical check. A formal assessment of capability leading to an operational declaration or combat ready status.

TAD. A tactical air direction radio frequency.

TWOATAF. Second Allied tactical Air Force.

Utils. The Utility hydraulic system.

WRAF. Women's Royal Air Force. An airwoman.

OTHER BOOKS BY THIS AUTHOR

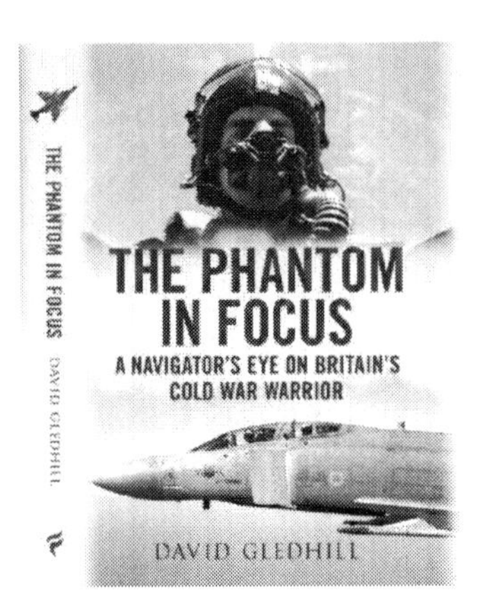

Have you ever wondered what it was like to fly the Phantom? This is not a potted history of an aeroplane, nor is it Hollywood glamour as captured in Top Gun. This is the story of life on the frontline during the Cold War told in the words of a navigator who flew the iconic jet. Unique pictures, many captured from the cockpit, show the Phantom in its true environment and show why for many years the Phantom was the envy of NATO. It also tells the inside story of some of the problems which plagued the Phantom in its early days, how the aircraft developed, or was neglected, and reveals events which shaped the aircraft's history and contributed to its demise. Anecdotes capture the deep affection felt by the crews who were fortunate enough to cross paths with the Phantom during their flying careers. The nicknames the aircraft earned were not complimentary and included the 'Rhino', 'The Spook', 'Double Ugly', the 'Flying Brick' and the 'Lead Sled'. Whichever way you looked at it, you could love or hate the Phantom, but you could never ignore it.

"The Phantom in Focus: A Navigator's Eye on Britain's Cold War Warrior" - ISBN 978-178155-048-9 (print) and ASIN B00GUNIM0Q (e-book) published by Fonthill Media.

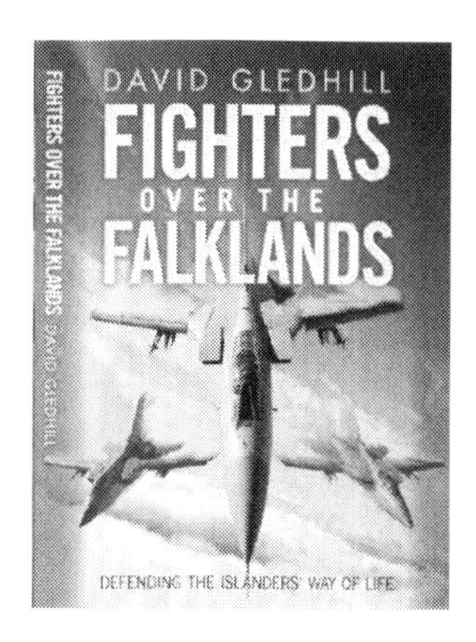

Fighters Over The Falklands: Defending the Islanders' Way of Life captures daily life using pictures taken during the author's tours of duty in the Falkland Islands. From the first detachments of Phantoms and Rapiers operating from a rapidly upgraded RAF Stanley airfield to life at RAF Mount Pleasant, see life from the author's perspective as the Commander of the Tornado F3 Flight defending the islands' airspace. Frontline fighter crews provided Quick Reaction Alert (QRA) during day to day flying operations working with the Royal Navy, Army and other air force units to defend a remote and sometimes forgotten theatre of operations. The book also examines how the islanders interacted with the forces based at Mount Pleasant and contrast high technology military operations with the lives of the original inhabitants, namely the wildlife.

"Fighters Over The Falklands – Defending the islanders Way of Life" - ISBN 978-17155-222-3 (print) and ASIN: B00H87Q7MS (e book) published by Fonthill Media.

The Tornado F2 had a troubled introduction to service. Unwanted by its crews and procured as a political imperative, it was blighted by failures in the acquisition system. Adapted from a multi-national design and planned by committee, it was developed to counter a threat which disappeared. Modified rapidly before it could be sent to war, the Tornado F3 eventually matured into a capable weapons system but despite datalinks and new air to air weapons, its poor reputation sealed its fate. The author, a former Tornado F3 navigator, tells the story from an insider's perspective from the early days as one of the first instructors on the Operational Conversion Unit, through its development and operational testing, to its demise. He reflects on its capabilities and deficiencies and analyses why the aircraft was mostly under-estimated by opponents. Although many books have already described the Tornado F3, the author's involvement in its development will provide a unique insight into this complex and misunderstood aircraft programme and dispel some of the myths. This is the author's 3rd book and, like the others, captures the story in pictures taken in the cockpit and around the squadron.

"Tornado F3 In Focus – A Navigator's Eye on Britain's Last Interceptor" - ISBN 978-178155-307-7 (print) and ASIN B00TM7A80E (e book) published by Fonthill Media.

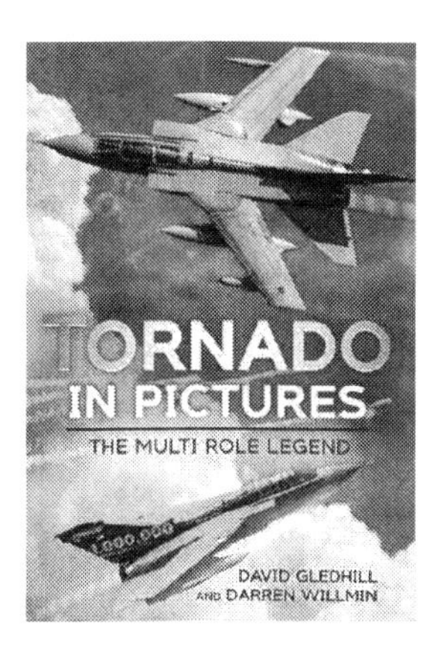

The Panavia Tornado was designed as a multi-role combat aircraft to meet the needs of Germany Italy and the United Kingdom. Since the prototype flew in 1974, nearly 1000 Tornados have been produced in a number of variants serving as a fighter-bomber, a fighter and in the reconnaissance and electronic suppression roles. Deployed operationally in numerous theatres throughout the world, the Tornado has proved to be exceptionally capable and flexible. From its early Cold War roles it adapted to the rigours of expeditionary warfare from The Gulf to Kosovo to Afghanistan. The early "dumb" bombs were replaced by laser-guided weapons and cruise missiles and in the air-to-air arena fitted with the AMRAAM and ASRAAM missiles.

In this book David Gledhill explores the range of capabilities and, having flown the Tornado F2 and F3 Air Defence Variant, offers an insight into life in the cockpit of the Tornado. Lavishly illustrated, Darren Wilmin's superb photographs capture the essence of the machine both from the ground and in the air. This unique collection including some of David Gledhill's own air-to-air pictures of the Tornado F2 and F3 will appeal to everyone with an interest in this iconic aircraft.

“Tornado In Pictures _ The Multi Role Legend” - ISBN 978-1781554630 (print) published by Fonthill Media.

Colonel Yuri Andrenev, a respected test pilot is trusted to evaluate the latest Soviet fighter, the Sukhoi Su27 "Flanker", from a secret test facility near Moscow. Surely he is above suspicion? With thoughts of defection in his mind, and flying close to the Inner German Border, could he be tempted to make a daring escape across the most heavily defended airspace in the world? A flight test against a Mig fighter begins a sequence of events that forces his hand and after an unexpected air-to-air encounter he crosses the border with the help of British Phantom crews. How will Western Intelligence use this unexpected windfall? Are Soviet efforts to recover the advanced fighter as devious as they seem or could more sinister motives be in play? Defector is a fast paced thriller which reflects the intrigue of The Cold War. It takes you into the cockpit of the Phantom fighter jet with the realism that can only come from an author who has flown operationally in the NATO Central Region.

"Defector" - ISBN 978-1-49356-759-1 (print) and ASIN B00EUYEUDK (e book) published by DeeGee Media. Defector is also available as an audiobook.

Combat veteran Major Pablo Carmendez holds a grudge against his former adversaries. Diverting his armed Skyhawk fighter-bomber from a firepower demonstration he flies eastwards towards the Falkland Islands intent on revenge. What is his target and will he survive the defences alerted of his intentions? Crucially, will his plan wreck delicate negotiations between Britain and Argentina designed to mend strained relations? Are Government officials charged with protecting the islanders' interests worthy of that trust or are more sinister motives in play? Maverick is an aviation thriller set in the remote outpost in the South Atlantic Ocean that takes you into the cockpits of the Phantom fighters based on the Islands where you will experience the thrills of air combat as the conspiracy unfolds.

"Maverick" - ISBN 978-1507801895 (print) and ASIN B00S9UL430 (e book) published by DeeGee Media.

When a hostage is snatched from the streets of Beirut by Hezbollah terrorists it sets in train a series of events from the UK to the Middle East that end in the corridors of power. A combined air operation is mounted from a base in Cyprus to release the agent from his enforced captivity. Phantom and Buccaneer crews help a special forces team to mount a daring raid, the like of which has not been attempted since Operation Jericho during World War 2. With Syrian forces ranged against them and Israeli and American friends seemingly bent on thwarting them, the outcome is by no means certain. As in his other novels David Gledhill takes you into the cockpit in this fast paced Cold War tale of intrigue and deception.

"Deception" - ISBN 978-1508762096 (print) and ASIN B00V8JTE40 (e book) published by DeeGee Media.

With tensions rising in post-war Europe, the Soviet Union closed the air corridors to Berlin, the former German capital, in a bid to starve the population into submission. The western allies responded by mounting the largest air supply operation the world had ever seen which would become known as the "Berlin Airlift".

Step forward into the 1980s with the Cold War at its height. A NATO reinforcement exercise held at a British airbase in West Germany, brings British, American and French fighter crews together to practice the air corridor policing mission. When a Pembroke transport aircraft engaged in a covert reconnaissance mission is intercepted by a Mig fighter and forced to land in East Germany, events escalate. Will the crew become a pawn in the relentless confrontation as the Soviets increase the rhetoric? Have western military plans been compromised by the unexpected aggression?

Provocation is a fast moving thriller that replays the tensions of the Cold War and its dark undertones. As with his other novels, David Gledhill takes you into the cockpit of the Phantom fighter jet to experience the action first hand.

"Provocation" - ISBN 978-1515382584 (print) and ASIN B014GUHGKG (e book) published by DeeGee Media. Provocation is also available as an audiobook.

Printed in Great Britain
by Amazon